Two Mothers

A Saigon Pilgrimage

Books by Linda Cardillo

Dancing on Sunday Afternoons

True Harvest

Two Mothers: A Saigon Pilgrimage

Across the Table

Love That Moves the Sun

Italian Tales

The Smallest Christmas Tree

First Light Series

The Boat House Café

The Uneven Road

Island Legacy

A Place of Refuge

Catríona's Vow

Two Mothers

A Saigon Pilgrimage

Linda Cardillo

Bellastoria
Press

Two Mothers

A Saigon Pilgrimage

ISBN: 978-1-959102-10-6

Second Edition

Previously published as *A Daughter's Journey*

BELLASTORIA PRESS

P.O. Box 60341

Longmeadow, Massachusetts 01116

In memory of Aaron Lazare

Part One

1975

The staccato tapping of the keys on Melanie Ames' portable Smith-Corona was echoed by the monsoon rains beating relentlessly on the tin roof of Mr. Bao's tea house across the alley from Mel's open window. Sweat dribbled down her neck below her cropped, dark brown hair as the ceiling fan cranked ineffectually above her, shoving the moist overheated air from one side of the cramped one-room flat to the other. Mel reached for another Marlboro from the pack in the breast pocket of her loose-fitting shirt. Close up, in the yellow pool of the light cast by the lamp on the table, one could see the slender wrists emerging from the sleeves of the shirt, the delicate bone structure of her face. But from a distance, as she moved in and out of the shadows in a disintegrating Saigon, the casual observer might not notice that she was a woman. It was one of the ways she protected herself. She defined it as making herself invisible, something she had learned as a young girl living abroad with her father on diplomatic missions. People tended not to notice or realize she was there because they didn't expect her to be. And thinking she was not there, they often said or did things she was not meant to hear or see.

She now used that talent in her profession as a journalist. People trusted her: bar girls in the noisy clubs that lined the teeming alleys of the city; shopkeepers; Navy lieutenants who ran river operations in the Delta; South Vietnamese army officers who talked to her over a beer and a cigarette.

Above the night voices of the rain and the ancient fan she heard the far-off reverberation of an explosion, then another. Despite the South Vietnamese government's insistence that it could defend Saigon, the word trickling through the city like the overrun sewers in the monsoon was that, as in Yeats' poem, the center would not hold.

Mel knew it was time to go. But after three years of writing about it, Vietnam was under her skin. Her pulse beat to the singsong rhythm of its language. And she knew she still had one more story to write in the mounting panic and confusion of impending loss.

Her journalism professor at Columbia had described it as fire in the belly. If you didn't have it, the burning desire to get the story no matter what the cost, you'd never make it in the news business. And Mel knew she had it.

As she hit the return on the typewriter and rolled out the thin sheet of paper with her latest story, she heard tapping on her door.

"Missy! Telephone call for you."

It was late, and there were few people left in Saigon close enough to her to call her here. She followed Mrs. Bao down the narrow stairs to the phone in the teahouse.

"Melly, this is Anh. I call because I have no one else to turn to. Please, I need your help."

Anh was a bar girl Mel had first met when she arrived in Saigon three years before. Where Mel had camouflaged her femininity to work and survive in Saigon, Anh had flaunted hers to the same end. Both had paid a price, and in that had found some common ground to ease the loneliness of life in a war zone, cut off from family. But Anh had dropped out of sight, and Mel hadn't seen her for over a year.

Her distress on the phone was palpable. She was insistent, a rising note of desperation in her voice that Mel had never heard before. Anh, the one with the veneer of bravado, the silken note of teasing promise, was voicing the despair whispered all over the city.

"I have to see you. Tonight. Can't talk on the phone."

Anh was working and Mel reluctantly agreed to meet her at the bar. She threw on a poncho and hurried the few blocks in the rain to meet her friend.

When she arrived she bought a drink for each of them to appease Anh's boss and Anh sat with her at a battered, sticky table. The place, once swarming with American servicemen and throbbing with Motown music, was nearly deserted.

Anh reached into her purse and pushed a photograph across the table to Mel. She looked at it, a smiling image of Anh in traditional Vietnamese dress (not the miniskirt and halter top that was her working outfit). In her arms was a baby.

"Who?" Mel asked.

"My daughter, Tien."

Mel knew that she and Anh had secrets, pieces of their lives they hadn't shared with one another. But this piece stunned her. Anh, at nineteen, was like a kid sister to twenty-three-year-old Mel. How could she not know Anh had a daughter?

"Where is she?"

"In the St. Agnes Orphanage on the outskirts of the city. I – I cannot care for her. Every month I send money. I thought, when I first left her there, it would be only until the end of the war. But now, I think there will be no end for me. That is why I am turning to you.

"I am thinking, if I can get her out of Vietnam to America, you can find her a family who would care for her. She is half American. She will have no life here."

"Does her father know about her?"

Anh shook her head. "He died before she was born."

"I don't know what I can do, Anh."

"You are smart, Melly. You have power – your boss in America, your father. Help me. I beg you. There is nothing I am asking for myself. Only for Tien. Please!"

Anh clutched Mel's hand, and in her touch Mel felt a force that she knew would stop at nothing to save her daughter. Mel had already witnessed that force in her friend.

Anh had once saved Mel's life. The first year she was in Saigon, Mel had made mistakes, not knowing whom to trust, where it was safe for a woman to walk alone. She'd been grabbed, dragged into an alley. Anh had seen her attacker, followed them, and put the knife she always carried against the attacker's throat, spewing a string of expletives and threats. The boy let go of Mel and ran.

It was after that experience that Mel cut her hair and took to wearing baggy clothes.

"What did you say to him?" Mel had asked her later, when Anh took her to her bar for a drink.

"I told him my pimp would cut his balls off."

It was after that experience that Mel cut her hair and took to wearing baggy clothes.

Mel knew she could not refuse to help.

"Take me tomorrow to St. Agnes. I'll see what I can do."

The next morning before she met Anh at the orphanage, Mel made some calls. She learned that some American agencies were indeed trying to arrange for adoptions of Vietnamese babies, especially those with American fathers. At least she could try to get Tien onto the list.

The morning rains had eased some when they arrived at St. Agnes. The woman at the door greeted Anh with a cold familiarity. It was clear to Mel that, while the children might be welcomed here, their mothers had earned only disapproval.

The stench of unchanged diapers assaulted Mel when the woman who had greeted them opened the door to Tien's ward. Two dozen cribs, most shared by two babies, filled the room. Mel saw a nun, harried but caring, moving from crib to crib changing diapers. It was quiet. No babbling or even crying followed them as they walked down the aisle to Tien's crib.

Anh reached for her daughter and murmured to her. The little girl, about six months old, was thin and pale, with dark eyes that moved solemnly from Anh to Mel and back again to her mother. She didn't smile in recognition, and Mel had no idea how often Anh had been able to visit.

They took the little girl to a small room where Anh bathed her and dressed her in fresh clothes she had brought with her. Then she fed her with some formula she'd asked Mel to buy.

"They do the best they can with so many children. But I know it's not enough. And can you imagine what they will face when the Americans are gone? You see why I have to get her out!"

Mel left Anh to spend a few more minutes alone with her daughter and wandered through the maze of rooms in the building that had once been one of the villas housing some expatriate merchant during the French occupation. Its former elegance was lost in the aging, dilapidated rooms now crowded with nearly four hundred children. Unlike the nursery, the rooms filled with older children echoed with the shouts and energy of kids cooped up after too many days of rain.

In one room she saw a small group clustered around a man chatting animatedly with them as he examined throats and listened to heart beats.

Mel was surprised to find a doctor. Behind her, the Mother Superior spoke, as if anticipating her question.

"He's Doctor Phillip Coughlin. One of your countrymen. An ex-Marine who came back to help us care for the children. He's a gift from God." Then with a wry smile, she added, "And he knows it."

With a swish of her skirts, she walked away.

Mel was waiting for Anh in the vestibule when Dr. Coughlin emerged like the Pied Piper, trailed by several of the children.

He stuck out his hand. "Phil Coughlin. Are you here to help?"

He flashed a smile, his brilliant blue eyes meeting her hazel ones with a direct and intense gaze. Mel imagined that he was one of those people who could walk into a room, address a crowd of people and have each one believe he was speaking only to him or her. He was arresting. But rather than finding it attractive, Mel was uncomfortable with his attention focused on her. She felt far too visible. Too vulnerable.

"No. Rather, I'm here to help one of the children. I'm trying to arrange for her adoption."

"Who the hell are you?" Coughlin's welcoming charm had been abruptly short-circuited.

"Mel Ames. *Newsweek* correspondent."

Coughlin was silent for a moment.

"I know your work," he said thoughtfully. It wasn't clear *what* he thought of her work, however.

"You're younger than I imagined. And I didn't know you were a woman."

Mel was used to both perceptions, but they still made her bristle. She had trained herself not to take the bait and simply smiled.

"You could do something more with that pen of yours, you know. You've got the talent, and you've probably got more of an audience than you realize."

She didn't like people telling her how to do her job. She was used to the military, the politicians telling her what she should write, how she should slant an article. She never listened to them. And she had no intention of listening to Phil Coughlin.

"You say you're trying to help one baby. Why that one? Why only one?"

"I've made a commitment to a friend to help her get her daughter on an adoption list. It's a personal request from someone I care about."

"You could save this whole orphanage."

"What are you talking about? You're as naïve as my friend. I don't even know if I can get *one* child out of here, let alone hundreds."

"You underestimate your own power. Or you are incredibly selfish, to see only the suffering of one you know and ignore the others."

"I've seen the others. I'm not blind to the need here."

"Then *do something* about it! Of all the people who have walked in here with their hearts on their sleeve bearing boxes of formula or clothing donated from their neighbors, you can do more with your words than a hundred of them!"

"What do you mean?"

"Tell the world about this place – and the tens of others in the city – caring for the children abandoned by their sons and shunned by their mothers' people. Tell the world."

And he walked away, dismissing her.

Despite her dislike of Phillip Coughlin and her resistance to being told what to do, Mel admitted to herself that rescuing one child was not enough. The already desperate conditions in the orphanage, coupled with the uncertain fate of the country, were overwhelming. She still doubted that her words alone could make a difference, but now that she had seen St. Agnes she didn't think she could forget it.

She spent the rest of the morning talking to the Reverend Mother, got a list of contacts and went to the *Newsweek* office in the Hotel Continental on Catinat Street to start making phone calls. She talked to adoption agencies, government officials, her editor in New York.

Within a few days she had accomplished her original mission—one of the agencies agreed to include Tien on its adoption list, provided Anh was willing to sign away her maternal rights. Mel found Anh at the bar that evening.

"Were you able to find a way to save Tien?" Anh's face was tight with hope.

Mel nodded and handed her friend the papers she would need to sign.

"Do you understand what this means? Relinquishing your rights to your daughter?"

"I have no choice, Melly. This is what I must do." She hesitated. "One more thing. I can still see her at St. Agnes, say goodbye?"

"I'm sure Reverend Mother wouldn't keep you away."

Anh's hand trembled as she put her signature on the pale yellow sheets Mel placed on the table. When she was done, she blew on the ink, quickly folded the papers and thrust them into Mel's hands.

"Take them away from me before I change my mind." She got up and strode away from Mel without looking back. At the bar she slid next to one of the few customers, whispered in his ear and then led him onto the dance floor.

As Mel left, she saw a vacant, haunted look in Anh's eyes as she melted into the stranger's embrace.

That night in her flat Mel pounded out her story—the desperate conditions in the orphanages, the excruciating choices and personal cost of the war to women like Anh, the thousands of children who were innocent victims and the individuals who were racing against the approaching North Vietnamese army to rescue them.

She had gotten permission from the Reverend Mother to bring a photographer to the orphanage and had managed to convince one of her *Newsweek* colleagues to take the photos. The next morning she sent the film and the story via courier to her editor in New York. She went back to her flat, thinking she was done.

But she was mistaken. In the short time that she had spent at St. Agnes, its children and the adults caring for them had affected her more than anyone else she had encountered in Vietnam. She found a reason every day to return to the orphanage—sometimes meeting Anh there as she spent her final days with her daughter and other times arriving with whatever she could scrounge from the dwindling number of expatriates in the city.

When her article appeared the following week, it set off an avalanche of concern for the orphans of Vietnam and launched an extraordinary concerted effort to rescue them. Mel was astounded. Her years in Vietnam had hardened the armor around her soul. What she had seen and reported on had accumulated and weighed upon her—young men with broken bodies and shattered minds; an unseen enemy hiding among the innocent; villages burned; trees stripped bare. She had not anticipated that this story of hers would have such impact.

Despite the hopeful activity that followed her story, Mel was suddenly plagued one night by nightmares. But rather than revisiting the horrors surrounding her in the city, her mind thrust her back to her childhood and the day her mother died giving birth to Mel's brain-damaged brother, David, when Mel was ten. Another dream placed her in her grandmother Dessie's house in Georgetown, abruptly pulled from her school in Bonn when her father, devastated by the loss of his wife, shut himself up in his work as a diplomat and took an assignment in the Congo.

The dreams woke Mel up in the middle of the night, the sweat seeping through her thin cotton tee-shirt caused by more than the oppressive heat. She reached for a cigarette and went out on the narrow balcony that overlooked the street. In the distance, to the north, she could see flashes of light, a phosphorescence that spread out in the mist.

How many days? She shook off the fears of the child who hadn't understood why she'd been left by first one and then the other parent. There were far more real fears only miles away.

Unable to go back to sleep, she paced until dawn, then dressed and hurried to the orphanage. She told herself with the firefight so near she wanted to make sure that Tien wasn't forgotten in what might be a chaotic departure.

She rang the ancient bell and waited for the shuffling feet of the night porter. The old woman's face registered surprise at Mel's presence on the crumbling doorstep, but let her in.

"Reverend Mother at matins," she announced. "Too early to speak to you."

"I'm not here for Reverend Mother. I came . . ."

Mel didn't know how to explain the urgency of her trip across the city. It occurred to her that the old woman might very well understand that Mel had been summoned by a dream, but she felt suddenly foolish.

"I came to help with the morning feedings." She finally uttered a reasonable excuse for her unorthodox arrival.

"Okay. Okay. Sister be very happy to see you. You know the way to the babies?"

Mel nodded and made her way across the cracked terrazzo floor to the nursery. Diapers that had been scrubbed so many times they were nearly transparent hung from lines stretched across one end of the room. The smell of urine mingled with sour milk hovered in the room. A single infant was crying and Mel hurried to Tien's crib.

But Tien was still asleep, curled in her corner of the crib, thumb in mouth.

Mel looked around. The sister in charge of the ward must also be at matins. The crying continued, persistent and building to a crescendo that Mel feared would soon wake the other babies. Her eyes scanned the cribs for the needy child and found him clutching the bars of his bed and banging his head against them.

She moved quickly, striding down the narrow aisle between the crammed metal cribs until she reached the screaming little boy. His diaper was soaked and full, and Mel could see little brown rivulets dripping down his legs. She hesitated.

Come on! You've seen a lot worse than this out in the field.

She reached into the crib and picked up the boy, holding him away from the front of her shirt. He abruptly stopped his wailing. Mel remembered a stone sink near the end of the room where the diapers were strung and moved toward it quickly.

She sat the boy in the sink. She turned the faucet and a trickle of water emerged, but it was enough. When he was clean, she lifted him again, holding him awkwardly with one arm while she grabbed a clean diaper from the line above her head. It had been a long time since she had held a baby. She remembered sitting very still when her grandmother had placed her infant brother in her waiting a rms.

"You have to support his head, Melanie. He can't hold it up by himself yet."

She had held her breath, afraid to move the elbow where David's oddly shaped head had rested. He hadn't been a squirming infant, but lay very still, no sign of recognition in his eyes. He looked like her mother.

The child now in her arms was twisting and kicking, his wet skin slippery. The unfamiliarity of this weight and shape against her body was unnerving.

I have no idea what I am doing.

She managed to sort out how to pin the diaper around him and then returned him to his crib, where to her relief he put his head down. She retreated to the sink, found a battered plastic bucket and filled it with water to soak the soiled diaper.

Other children were beginning to stir, although Tien still slept. Mel thought about leaving the nursery, finding some pretext for taking out her notebook. But she stayed, and as babies woke up she repeated the bathing and diapering.

Mel was at the sink rinsing diapers when she saw Phil Coughlin in the doorway at the opposite end of the room, stethoscope around his neck and a small piece of paper in his hand. Mel was surprised that he'd be here at such an early hour. He looked as if he'd had as sleepless a night as she'd had, but she guessed it hadn't been nightmares that had kept him awake. His skin had the gray pallor of too many hours spent in smoke-filled bars and he hadn't shaved. She assumed he'd come directly from whatever nightclub was still serving the remnants of the American community still in Saigon. She'd heard a few stories about Phil Coughlin since the day he directed her to write about the orphans. A couple of the Marines guarding the Embassy had served with him a few years before.

"Phil Coughlin? Man, that guy was a wild man in town. Everybody knew if you were looking for a party, just put a tail on Coughlin and he'd lead you to it. But on duty, there was nobody else in the Corps I'd rather have putting me back together when I got hit. I've seen the guy under fire, hands steady as a robot, blood from a severed artery pumping all over him and he kept the grunt alive. Saved his leg, too."

"What's he doing back in Nam? I was at his farewell party last August. He was joking about some plush job in Boston he had lined up – he was going to be the doc to some big-shot politician's family."

"Why would anybody come back?"

No one Mel talked to had the answer to that question and it was unlikely Phil Coughlin would answer it himself. Her contact with him since the day she'd met him at St. Agnes had been limited to seeing him surrounded by children clamoring for his attention.

From her end of the room, Mel now watched Phil approach one of the cribs and examine a tiny girl with pale, almost blue skin and a bloated belly. She noted how deftly and gently he touched the child, in sharp contrast to Mel's own clumsy grasping of the squirming children she'd been bathing. He made some notations on the slip of paper as Sister Agatha, the nun in charge of the nursery, rushed in.

"I didn't expect you so early, Dr. Coughlin. Matins were delayed because we were waiting for Father Joseph to bring communion."

She was tying a gingham apron around her gray habit as she spoke and pulled a notepad from the pocket. She took a position at his side as they stopped at the beds of the sickest children.

Mel, sweaty and damp, her shirt stained from too many equally damp babies pressed against her, considered easing herself quietly out of the nursery. She suddenly felt like an intruder, an interloper in the domain of those with a far more important mission. She imagined Phil Coughlin would certainly perceive her that way (although Sister Agatha, she hoped, would appreciate the freshly diapered babies, however awkwardly it had been accomplished).

Mel was in no mood for another of Coughlin's condescending remarks. Despite her constant activity and the repetitive, mind-numbing nature of bathing and changing the children, she hadn't dispelled the unease that her nightmares had precipitated. If anything, the work of the last hour had only amplified her sense of the desperation in the orphanage – not only the physical limitations of the crumbling building and its insufficient supplies, but the emotional deprivation of the children. Sister Agatha, as efficient and compassionate as she had to be, was only one person. The babies barely cried because they had learned that no one responded to their cries. They withdrew into a realm of isolation, staring at the patterns of light and shadow made by their own hands.

Mel's brother David had done that. No cooing or smiling or returns of affection. Just a blankness and emptiness where she had hoped to find an emerging personality, a brother who would love her. But in addition to his damaged brain, David was also physically frail. When he was four his congenitally weakened heart had simply stopped, and he was gone.

Mel shook off the brooding memory. She didn't dwell on losses; life threw too many at you. Soldiers who had shared a shot and a beer on a humid night returning the next day in a body bag; her father receding from her life as he spiraled deeper into his work, unable to recover from his own losses; the boyfriend at Columbia who had resented her winning the *Newsweek* assignment, accusing her of taking a spot that she didn't deserve.

"First of all, you'll never get the kind of stories a man would be able to write. There are places you can't go, people who won't talk to you because you're a woman. And second, even if you're able to get the experience, it'll be wasted on you. You'll come back after a couple of years, get married and decide to stay home with your kids."

Mel had no intention of having children. Her mother's death giving birth to David had sealed that decision. But she didn't tell her boyfriend that. She didn't want to waste her breath trying to justify why she was as deserving as a man to be writing for *Newsweek*. But it was after his resentment surfaced that she decided to use Mel for her byline, not Melanie.

Each of those losses had felt like someone had punched her in the belly, knocking the breath out of her. She had wanted no more of caring so deeply about anyone that their loss could cause her pain.

She cautioned herself not to allow her concern for the plight of the children of St. Agnes to drag her back to the vulnerability and weakness she had put behind an impenetrable wall of detachment.

She was thinking too much – an observation her grandmother had often made about her growing up. So she thrust herself back into activity. If she kept moving and doing, she distracted herself from such thoughts. That was why she had left her flat so early this morning, driven from the unnamed fears in her bed. There was little in Saigon to occupy her now except the orphans.

She slipped out of the nursery before she had to speak to Coughlin.

On her way back to the front of the house she encountered a girl of about seven.

"Reverend Mother heard you are here. She's looking for you."

Mel followed the girl. She didn't particularly want to be pulled into the superior's circle. Whenever she had seen her, the nun peppered Mel with questions, demanding information she thought Mel had access to. Mel couldn't blame her. The woman, like everyone else in Saigon, was desperate for whatever fragments she could glean to protect her charges.

But this time it was Reverend Mother who had information for her.

Reverend Mother was just returning the phone's receiver to its cradle. Mel saw that her hand was trembling.

"Something has happened." Mel was certain.

The nun's face crumpled in anguish.

"The first planeload of children left Tan Son Nhut this morning. It crashed shortly after takeoff."

Mel felt the nun's words as if a grenade had torn through her chest. She gripped the desk and leaned toward the nun.

"Survivors?" She could barely speak the word.

"We don't know. I got the call from Madame Deng. The children were from her orphanage. They were supposed to be the lucky ones to get out first. She was watching from the terminal.

"I have experienced more than my share of horror in my life, Miss Ames. God has granted me the strength and the will to lift a child bloodied but unharmed from under the body of her mother, who threw herself over her child to protect her. And I've accepted babies from their mothers who cannot return to their families with a dark-skinned child.

"I thought we were doing the right thing – your story, the outpouring of concern, the airlift. How can it be that we are putting these babies in harm's way by trying to bring them to safety?"

She seized Mel's hand, her grip at once both powerful and needy.

"We cannot be deterred by this catastrophe, Miss Ames. We can grieve, we can pray for the souls of those on board. But we cannot stop. You must let the world know that."

At that moment Phil Coughlin burst into the room.

"I just heard. They'll need assistance at Tan Son Nhut if there are any survivors. Ames, if you're finished changing diapers, come with me."

Reverend Mother released her hand. "Do what you can," she said. Behind her wire-rimmed glasses, Mel saw tears welling up in the nun's eyes.

Coughlin grabbed his black bag and Mel followed, adrenaline kicking in after the horror of what she had just learned. She forced herself to ignore his deprecating remark about the diapers. She knew her usefulness in the nursery was limited. There was no need for him to rub it in.

But at the airport she'd be in her element. Amidst the chaos she knew would greet them, she'd find her way. Coughlin was simply a means to get there, and she put aside her anger that he had ordered her to come with him. Once a Marine, she thought, having been at the receiving end of far too many comments intended to intimidate her.

She wasn't expecting their mode of transportation to be a Vespa scooter. Somehow she thought the esteemed doctor would have had access to a Jeep. Reluctantly, she climbed on behind him. At first she gripped the seat, but his speed as he wove through the crowded streets forced her to clasp her arms around his waist.

She hadn't been this close to a man in a long time. She could smell the bite of his sweat, hear the shallow pant of his breathing, feel the accelerated beating of his heart. The intensity of his physical response to the news they had heard echoed hers. She tried to calm herself and prepare for what she knew awaited them at the airport. But she was too aware of Coughlin – his restlessness, his impatience as he raced toward the crash. She hated the sensations rippling through her and pushed them aside. She felt sucked in by him in ways she had never experienced before, and she didn't like it.

When they arrived at Tan Son Nhut, she leapt off the scooter, eager to distance herself from his intensity. But he grabbed her by the hand.

"You won't get through without me, so stick close. If anyone asks, you're a nurse, not a journalist."

She followed him reluctantly, acknowledging that he was right. An agitated mob, witnesses to the crash, pushed up against the chain link fence. Some women were wailing, clawing their way through the crowd, while others stood off on a small rise in a state of profound grief, stunned and motionless. In the distance, beyond the end of the runway, Mel could see billowing clouds of dense black smoke. Sirens wailed.

She plunged forward with Coughlin, his arm now tightly around her, as they made their way to the securely guarded entrance to the terminal. The soldiers were letting no one through except rescue personnel, their faces grim with the strain of holding back the distraught crowd, their weapons raised and ready.

Mel kept her mouth shut with difficulty as she listened to Coughlin, a civilian without authority over them, talk the soldiers into letting the two of them beyond the checkpoint. Even though the soldiers didn't know him, they knew *of* him. But it was more than his reputation – part of which she realized she was responsible for, thanks to including him in her article. The image of a frail child in the arms of the handsome, blue-eyed doctor had been beamed around the world. His vivid commentary had had as much impact as any of her descriptions of the severe plight of the orphans.

"Sergeant, I'm Doctor Phil Coughlin, retired Marine Corps, and the physician to the children who were on that flight. If any of them are still alive, I need to be at their side. I know you understand that. I also know you have orders and if I need to speak to your C.O to give me permission to proceed, I'm more than happy to do that."

Phil flashed them a smile. Rather than intimidate them, he was professing to understand their position while expecting them to recognize his moral authority. Mel grudgingly admitted that his moral authority was authentic. He cared deeply about those children and believed himself responsible for their very lives.

Mel knew that, had she been alone, she would have been her scrappy, combative, persistent self. She hadn't gotten as far as she had in the few short years she'd been a journalist by making nice to all the people who told her, "No, you can't go there."

But Coughlin displayed a muted self-confidence, absolutely convinced that he had a right to be on the tarmac saving "his" children. Apparently, he convinced the guards as well.

"There's no need to contact the C.O., sir. I have the discretion to let someone as significant as you onto the compound."

"Thank you, Sergeant, in the name of the children."

And with that, Mel and Coughlin were waved through. Once inside the terminal they raced onto the airstrip and grabbed a ride with one of the emergency vehicles heading toward the site of the crash.

The stench of burning aircraft fuel and the thickening smoke engulfed them. Mel looked over at Coughlin and saw that the charming smile had disappeared. In its place was an emotional barrier as opaque as if he had tied on a surgical mask. His whole body leaned forward, poised as if ready to pounce on an attacker.

When the rescue truck came to a halt at the edge of a marsh, Coughlin jumped out, his eyes scanning the smoke-filled, boggy area for signs of activity. He shouted to Mel to stay close.

"I need your help here, Ames. I didn't bring you along so that you could score another journalistic coup. I've already handed you your Pulitzer Prize on a silver platter. Now it's time to get your hands dirty."

"I think I've already earned that stripe," Mel shouted back. She wasn't looking for a story now. She was looking for signs of life.

All around them was chaos – the choking smells, the sounds of screams, the swarm of rescuers trying to get close to the plane, the pulsing of foam cannons on the fire trucks smothering the flames.

Coughlin wove his way through a staggered line of soldiers aiming hoses at the wreckage to a clearing where Mel could see a pile of stretchers near a van emblazoned with a red cross. When they reached the stretchers she could see that they were empty.

The control and focus that seemed to be propelling Coughlin since they had left the orphanage slipped for a few seconds. Mel caught a glimpse of what she took to be despair behind the mask. She began to tremble, absorbing Coughlin's realization as if it were her own. Were there no survivors? She couldn't accept that. Something possessed her – an outrage that she couldn't quell; a surge of unfamiliar strength and invincibility.

She plunged farther into the smoke-filled bog toward what she thought were voices. She couldn't see more than a few feet ahead of her, but she kept moving toward shouts and the frail but definite sound of a child's cry.

She nearly wept when she stumbled into a soldier carrying a child – not the body of a child, but a breathing, screaming child. He thrust the baby into her arms.

"There are more. Parts of the plane are still intact. We're trying to get them out."

Beyond him she could see children being passed from one set of arms to another.

"We're trying to get them away from the plane in case the rest of it blows. Tell the medics in the clearing we've got survivors."

He turned back to the plane.

Mel ran with the baby. Coughlin had followed her and met her halfway to the clearing.

"Survivors coming" she choked out the words. The despair she had seen in his eyes had disappeared. It its place was something else. Not just relief that some of his children might be alive, but a grudging respect that was directed at her. He took the baby from her and held her gaze long enough for her to absorb that it was meant for her.

She turned back toward the plane to retrieve another child, distracted by the effect Coughlin was having on her. It was as if he had swallowed her emotionally. Each shift in his mood was reverberating through her. She'd been close enough to exploding mines before to have felt the shock waves, and that was what she now compared to the sensations coursing through her. Dangerous. Overpowering.

She steadied herself both physically and emotionally and concentrated on the task ahead of her, forcing herself to act with purpose as the noise and confusion of the rescue mounted. The mud of the bog sucked at her feet and slowed the movements of everyone trying to evacuate the shattered fuselage. She joined a ragged line that was passing babies from the wreckage back to the hastily organized triage area where Coughlin was.

She had no doubt that he had established himself at the center of that operation as soon as she had handed him the first baby. Mel kept her thoughts on moving the children to safety and medical treatment and tried desperately not to react to what was being put in her arms – the bloodied, frail bodies, most of the children in shock. Out of some long forgotten memory, she began singing a lullaby she had learned from her grandmother to calm David when he'd been restless. Someone had dumped a pile of blankets at her feet and she wrapped each child handed to her, crooning to them as she carried the almost weightless bundles to the medics.

Ambulances were arriving and leaving in a steady stream, carrying the most severely injured away. Stretchers had been brought to the wreckage for the adults on the flight. Like the faces of the children, theirs were dazed, stressed, looks of profound disbelief and confusion staring out at their rescuers. Some of them held babies in their arms and Mel couldn't tell if they were alive or not.

She kept putting one foot in front of another, not stopping to process what she was observing, what she herself was experiencing. She had lost track of Coughlin and that was just as well. It was a relief not to be so aware of him. His presence earlier had been a hot breath on her neck, an unwelcome pressure on her heart.

When it was clear that there were no more survivors, Mel's attention shifted to the triage area. Children needed to be held as IVs were inserted; extra hands were called for to stem bleeding or grab supplies.

It was hours before the last ambulance left the marsh. Body bags were lined up, waiting to be picked up and delivered to a temporary morgue. The chaos and noise of the rescue had given way to a hollow emptiness as the enormity of what had occurred began to seep through the clearing. The adrenaline that had been sustaining everyone was rapidly diminishing, and with its loss came the exhaustion and pain that had been held at bay throughout the day.

Mel's head jolted up with the roar of a plane taking off again from Tan Son Nhut. She could hear shelling to the north and realized it must have been going on as always. Time had been frozen for her, and she had believed that all else had stopped around her. The understanding that the world had gone on while she had been in the middle of a nightmare filled her with loneliness. Who would understand what she had experienced today, what she had lived through in the last three years?

She felt a hand on her shoulder and was too numb to even flinch.

"You're going to need a ride home. I asked one of the MPs to bring my Vespa up here from the terminal."

He pointed to the muddy scooter leaning against the wheel of a truck.

She was going to refuse, not willing to put herself once again in close contact with him. But she was bone tired, and a quick glance around convinced her she'd have to search awhile for transportation. Reluctantly, she followed him to the bike.

"You surprised me today, Ames. Usually the members of the fourth estate around here are merely observers – and not very accurate ones. You also held it together pretty well, for all that you saw. As far as I could tell, nobody had to hold your head while you lost your breakfast."

"I had no breakfast to lose," Mel answered. It no longer surprised her that, even in apparently complimenting her he managed to dismiss her because of her profession. As far as she could tell, Phil Coughlin was willing to see some slight value in journalism only when it suited his own ends.

She'd save lives today, damn it, not holding a pen in her hand but cradling barely breathing children and bearing them to safety. Why did Phil Coughlin's grudging acknowledgment of what she'd done chafe so much? She tried to attribute her vulnerability to fatigue and hunger. But she sensed that these feelings, however unwelcome, were not going to disappear with a meal and a night's rest.

"We both could use something to eat, not to mention a shot of Scotch. There's a noodle shop a few doors from my flat. I'll buy you dinner."

He pushed down on the kick-starter and they took off into the dusk, Mel's "No thanks," muffled by the low rumble of the bike.

She had no idea where Coughlin lived, but hoped it was near enough to her own neighborhood to get home under her own power. She was more tired than she realized and found herself leaning against his back, damp with sweat and reeking of the fumes that had billowed from the wreckage. It should have been off-putting in many ways, but there was a familiarity and comfort that tugged at her and she didn't pull back. She caught a glimpse of herself in his side mirror. Her face was streaked with soot and her shirt, already christened from the diaper changing early that morning, now bore witness to the hell she had thrashed through in the marshes. She wanted a bath; she wanted a hot bowl of noodles; she wanted her bed, however haunted it had been the night before.

The night before. How long ago that was! The dreams that had disturbed her now seemed childish and embarrassing compared to the true nightmare the orphans today had suffered through. Her reverie came to an abrupt halt as the motorbike skidded to a stop in a narrow alley somewhere in District 1.

The stop threw her off balance, thrusting her closer to Coughlin. She stayed that way a few seconds longer than she meant to, aware of her breasts beneath the loose-fitting shirt pressed against his back. Realizing what she'd done, she released herself from her hold around him and quickly jumped off the bike, turning her head away so that he wouldn't see how red her face was. Not from embarrassment, but from anger with herself. How could she be throwing her body at him – a man who seemed to find her as annoying and useless as she found him insufferable. She needed to get a grip on herself, get some food into her belly and get home.

She ignored the soft smile on Coughlin's face as he pushed open the rickety screen door to the noodle bar. With dismay, Mel saw that it had no tables – not even a counter with stools. It was take-out only. She'd thought this was going to be simple – a bowl of noodles surrounded by other diners who also looked upon the meal as no more than necessary nourishment, not as a social engagement. But now she had to add to her already overwhelmed brain the question of where she and Coughlin were going to eat.

That worry was replaced for a few minutes by the aromas drifting from the bubbling pots on the stove in the corner of the cramped and crowded shop. Coughlin steered her to the front, his touch on her arm as deft and gentle as the one she had observed in the nursery that morning at the orphanage. Nevertheless, her skin where his fingers rested prickled, as if Fourth of July sparklers were shedding their sparks. Dessie had always procured a small supply every summer when Mel had been a girl and her grandmother had lit them for her on the beach in front of their cottage on Martha's Vineyard. She had loved to hold one in each hand and wave them in wide arcs, watching the trail of white light float through the night air. Sometimes the sparks fell on her bare toes and she danced the tiny pricks of heat away.

She could not dance away from Phil Coughlin's heat tonight.

Instead, she nodded at the vegetable pot, refused the fish and watched without words but with a suddenly grumbling stomach as Mrs. Ling ladled her choices into battered tin pots with lids and handles. Phil let go of Mel to pay Mrs. Ling and take the pots. Mel followed him out of the shop and the question loomed again about where they would share this meal. If she had paid attention to the route Phil had taken from Tan Son Nhut instead of burying her head against him, she might recognize where she was, take her pot and walk or flag down a cycle taxi.

But the alley looked like dozens of others she'd wandered through.

"My place is just around the corner. If you take the noodles, I'll walk the bike. I've got a bottle of Glenlivet and even two clean glasses in the cupboard."

He handed her the steaming pots and she followed him as he guided the bike through the puddles in the alley to a small padlocked shed. He pulled a key from his pocket, unlocked the door and rolled the bike into the dirt-floored space. In the rear corner Mel could see neatly stacked boxes marked with red crosses.

Phil followed her glance.

"Medical supplies I've managed to scrounge. As I need them I deliver them to the orphanage but there's little left – just what you see there."

He closed up, took the pots and led her up an external flight of wooden stairs to a landing above the shed. He flicked on a light as he opened the door and Mel followed him inside.

The room they entered was starkly neat. A small counter held a hot plate and a line of canned goods. On shelves underneath were a small stack of plates and a couple of pots. A desk flanked the one window and on its surface Mel saw a well-thumbed copy of a *Physician's Desk Reference* and a few medical textbooks. Through a doorway hung with a bamboo curtain Mel saw a mosquito-netted bed.

"I've actually got a bathroom if you want to clean up before we eat."

He set the pots on a table in the middle of the room and pointed toward the bedroom.

"It's through here. I'll get you a towel and can offer you some clean clothes." His glance moved down from her face to her blood and grime-spattered shirt.

"You probably will want to burn that."

He led the way to the bath and handed her a towel, shirt and shorts.

"There's a tub if you want to soak. I can reheat the noodles when you're ready. Do you want a drink now or later?"

She turned down the drink and looked with longing at the claw-footed tub in the middle of the bath. This wasn't what she'd intended, but her flat had only a tiny box of a shower. She turned on the tap and peeled off her clothes while she waited for the tub to fill. When she finally eased herself into the warm water she could not imagine wanting to be anywhere else.

After she had scrubbed the vestiges of the day from her weary body she leaned back and let herself drift for a few minutes . . .

The knock was insistent, rapid.

"Melanie? Melanie, are you OK?" She heard genuine concern in his voice. And he had called her Melanie. Not Ames, which was the only way he had ever addressed her; and not Mel, which was how she referred to herself since she'd become a journalist. Only Dessie and her father called her Melanie.

She roused herself with a splash and rose from the tub.

"I'm fine. Sorry to alarm you. I'll be out in a minute."

She toweled herself dry, turbaned her hair and slipped on the crisply starched khaki shirt he had given her. The shorts came to her knees and were loose around the waist, so she slipped her belt off her own mud-caked pants and cinched the shorts tightly to keep them up.

Her fingertips and toes were wrinkled, but every inch of her was clean and smelled of Ivory soap. She was aware of his appraisal as she emerged from the bathroom.

"Now, that's an improvement. The noodles are on the hotplate. I'm going to wash up myself – be back a little faster than you were." And he ducked into the bath.

In the outer room she found the table set with bowls and spoons. An empty glass etched with Marine Corps insignia stood at one place with the promised bottle of Glenlivet next to it. She had noticed that Phil had taken his own glass into the bath.

She poured herself a splash of Scotch and swirled it around the glass, breathing in the aroma. Glenlivet had been her father's drink and Dessie had kept a crystal decanter on a silver tray on the sideboard in the dining room at Georgetown, ready and waiting for his sporadic returns from whatever hot spot he'd been assigned to solve its crises. Mel remembered him on those nights when he first came home – the quick, stiff hug in the front hall and then the step back from her to assess how much she'd grown or to note the presence, and later absence, of her braces; the kiss to the cheek Dessie offered him; and then the retreat to the dining room. Mel sat and watched her father, hungry for his presence, as he sank into his chair at the head of the table, loosened his tie and clasped the double rocks glass. He drank slowly, his eyes closed at first, each sip easing the creases of worry and fatigue that to Mel seemed deeper each time he returned.

Mel wondered now if her father's Glenlivet had helped to obliterate the horrors that had assaulted him on his missions. She'd seen enough hard drinking during her years in Saigon to understand how many men used it as an anesthetic. More than likely, from what she'd heard about Phil, it was his drug of choice.

She took a small sip, the gold liquid searing her throat and then warming her empty belly. She rubbed the bridge of her nose. Too much of this and she wouldn't be able to hold onto the motorbike, much less find her own way back to her flat.

She stifled a yawn as Phil parted the bamboo curtain and stepped back into the front room. He brought the pots to the table and ladled noodles and broth into her bowl.

"Eat, before you topple over."

They ate silently, hunger and weariness overtaking any attempt on either part to be sociable. Like the bath, the food met a need so basic that it quelled the earlier disquiet Mel had felt about being with Phil any longer than absolutely necessary. She swallowed the noodles and shredded cabbage voraciously, registering the warmth, the flecks of hot chili pepper, the intense flavors of garlic and onion and basil from the broth that must have been simmering for days.

"Thank you," she was finally able to murmur when her bowl was empty. "I hadn't realized how much I needed to eat."

She pushed her chair back from the table.

"I'll help you clean up and then I should get back to my place. If you'll sketch out for me where we are, I can walk or hail a cycle taxi."

"It's late and, if you haven't noticed, it's pouring out. It's not safe for you to head out by yourself. I'd take you on the bike, but after finally being clean and dry I suspect that both of us would regret the ride.

"Look, you can stay here. Take the bed. I'll camp out here on the couch. I need to be close to the phone anyway. The Seventh Adventist Hospital, where most of the survivors were taken, has my number. I spoke to them while you were in the tub. If they need me, I'll be on my way. It's another reason for me not to take you back to your flat – I don't want to miss their call."

"I can certainly travel on my own at night. I've been doing it for a long time."

"I imagine that you haven't been doing it when the city is streaming with desperate refugees from the north and today, especially, in the aftermath of the crash, when rumors are careening from one end of Saigon to the other. Stay put. It's not a suggestion. You'll be no good for your precious Tien if you're abducted or worse. There's mortar fire hitting the fringe of the city."

Phil's reversion to his "I'm in charge, don't mess with me" mode of communicating with her caught Mel off guard. Had he really been kind and solicitous earlier, or had she simply been lulled into thinking so by her fatigue and hunger? Under normal circumstances, Mel would never had allowed herself to be in this situation – dependent on a man who thought he knew what was best for her. Under normal circumstances, she would pick herself up and go, rain and mortar fire and panic in the streets be damned.

But she knew herself well enough to acknowledge that she was close to physical collapse. Whatever had driven her through this horrific day was gone. She bit back words that she knew might only fuel Phil's sense of her weakness and vulnerability. And she reluctantly admitted to herself how right he was with the clinching words of his argument to keep her at his place for the night. She had a responsibility beyond herself to Tien, a duty to fulfill to Anh.

"Fine. I'll stay. But I'll be on my way with first light."

She picked up the dishes and carried them to the bath, where she had seen a dishpan, sponge and incongruous container of Palmolive dishwashing liquid stowed under the sink. She washed and dried the dishes while Phil placed another call to the hospital.

When she was finished she found him making the bed.

"Clean sheets. You're all set for the night. Get some rest."

He left her and she climbed into the bed. Like the rest of his flat, the bedroom was almost monastic in its simplicity and starkness. The bed was narrow, not something she had expected, given Phil's carousing reputation. But then, he may have carried on that part of his life in other beds, rather than bringing women home to what appeared to Mel to be a sanctuary.

Next to the bed Mel found a stack of books on the night table. As tired as she was, as depleted of nearly all her resources, the journalist in her couldn't resist investigating. She ran her fingers along the spines: Thoreau's *On Walden Pond*; Julian of Norwich's *Revelations of Divine Love*; and Faulkner's *The Sound and the Fury*. She had expected Ian Fleming or Ed McBain, but was beginning to understand that what she had previously expected of Phil Coughlin and what she was discovering about him were worlds apart.

She had read Julian of Norwich at Columbia and began to leaf through the pages. Marginal notes in deep blue ink and a jagged, angular handwriting were scattered throughout the well-thumbed book. She was filled with a profoundly curious urge to read the notes, seeking some insight into why Phil Coughlin was so disturbingly compelling. It might give her some edge in dealing with him; provide her with some understanding of him with which to defend herself. Protect herself. But she hadn't read more than a few words, straining to decipher the script in the dim light of the single lamp by the bed, when her eyes and her brain simply refused to perform for even a few more minutes. Her head fell heavy into the pillow, the book sprawled open across her chest and she was asleep.

But it wasn't a restful sleep. Jumbled images of the smoke-filled bog; the broken fuselage; scattered limbs; her father's distant, sorrow-lined face; and Coughlin's intense blue eyes crowded her subconscious, accompanied by a cacophony of sirens and explosions and fragments of the lullaby she had sung as she carried the babies. She was lost in the smoke, the mud immobilizing her feet. She was hearing the cries of a child in the distance but couldn't reach her, despite struggling with every ounce of her strength. Panic rose in her and guilt, as the screams continued and she was helpless to stop them. She was frantic, clawing at her feet to dig out of the mud, but when she lifted her hands they were filled with blood.

Suddenly, cool hands grasped her own heated ones and a voice she couldn't see because of the smoke spoke to her calmly.

"Melanie. Melanie, it's only a dream. You're safe."

She struggled for a moment and then the bog and the smoke vanished, replaced by yellow light and an unrecognizable room. Where was she? The voice whispered to her.

"It's OK, Melanie. You're with me, Phil."

She opened her eyes and stared into his startlingly blue ones. He was sitting on the edge of the bed, stroking her still trembling hands.

"You must have had a bad dream – no surprise given what you witnessed today."

What she had witnessed flooded back and crushed her emotionally. She began to cry, keening as if she were one of her Irish aunts on her mother's side, mourning each of the shattered lives flung across the path of this war.

Phil took her face in his hands, wiping her tears with his thumbs, and then pulled her into an embrace, his arms wrapped around her as her body heaved with uncontrolled sobs. She emptied herself into him and he simply held her, absorbing her grief. When her tears subsided, he brushed her damp hair away from her face.

"Try to get some rest now. It's almost morning and you'll be needed at the orphanage. I'll stay here with you, if you want me to."

She nodded, not willing to be separated from the steadying rhythm of his heart, the strength in his arms holding her up and keeping further nightmares at bay.

She settled down again onto the narrow bed and he slipped behind her, her back leaning into his chest. His arm reached around her and clasped her hand.

"Sleep," he said. "I'm here."

When she woke a few hours later she could see faint cracks of light through the blinds on the window. She groped for her clock, a small, leather-bound travel clock that her father had given her when she left for Vietnam. It was the last time she had seen him. But the clock wasn't there, and the room and the bed weren't hers. She sat up with a start, remembering where she was and vaguely aware of the disturbance during the night. She was alone in the bed. Perhaps Phil coming to her in the midst of her dream had been part of the dream as well.

She wasn't sure which version of the night before upset her more – that her subconscious had been so consumed with him that he could be so present in her dreams; or that he had physically comforted her and she had welcomed him into her bed. But she had slept, wrapped in a cocoon of safety that he had somehow provided her.

She heard the water running in the bathroom and scrambled out of the bed. She didn't want to still be there in the midst of rumpled sheets if, indeed, he had held her and slept with her.

In the front room she found a pot of coffee on the hot plate and poured herself one of the thick ceramic Boston Red Sox mugs on the counter. Some caffeine and a cigarette would clear her fuzzy thinking. Whatever had happened the night before was an aberration, thrust upon her by the crash. She couldn't even remember the last time she had cried or needed comforting. She hadn't been herself, Mel Ames, seasoned war correspondent, that was all. She nearly dropped the mug when Phil entered the room behind her and spoke. He didn't have to touch her to evoke what convinced her now had definitely been a physical, not imagined experience. His voice held the same compassionate tone she remembered.

"You're up, and looking like your old self! I'm glad."

Mel realized with relief that he wasn't going to bring up the night spent entwined in his arms or even refer to her nightmare. For a fraction of a second he held her gaze when she turned to answer him. Our secret, his mesmerizing eyes seemed to promise. No need to ever mention it again. She hoped she could trust him.

"If you want a ride to the orphanage, I'm headed to that part of town. It's on the way to the hospital."

"Have you heard any more news?"

"No. That's why I'm going to stop by and see for myself."

"You'll let me now if there's anything I can do? Write another Pulitzer Prize-winning article?" She flashed him a wan grin. I'm still a journalist, she was saying. Despite last night.

He nodded.

Twenty minutes later he dropped her at the steps to the orphanage and waved goodbye.

When he was out of sight she turned in the opposite direction and headed toward the *Newsweek* office. She knew from the previous day the nursery would still be quiet. She had at least an hour before Tien and the other infants would be stirring.

She walked briskly. In alleys and under makeshift shelters she could see the sleeping bodies of those who must have fled the north. Dogs wandered the streets sniffing at garbage. Somewhere in the distance, a siren wailed.

She let herself into the deserted office, pulled the cover off a Teletype machine and sat down. Without benefit of notes, Mel began a firsthand account of the rescue. The senior byline writers in the bureau would be doing investigative pieces, confirming the rumors of sabotage that had floated above the smoke and despair in the marsh. But they hadn't been where she had been, mired in the mud, an eyewitness at the point of impact.

The words came quickly, images and vignettes pouring out of her brain as if exorcised by the act of telling. When she finished, she realized she was sweating. The story was on its way to New York when the first of her colleagues arrived.

"Where were you yesterday, Ames? All hell was breaking loose – at least, more than the usual chaos – and I didn't have anybody to get me the specs on that C-5A that went down. Did you start the coffee yet?"

Mel put the cover back on the Teletype. Despite earning her own byline at the magazine on the strength of her reporting over the last three years, the older reporters still treated her like their research assistants.

"Didn't have time, Joe. Gotta run. Doing some follow-up on the orphan story. The background on the C-5A is probably in the Lockheed file. The 'L's' are in the second drawer."

She picked up her knapsack and slipped past him, trying not to react to the chagrin registering on his face.

As she hurried back to the orphanage she could see the refugees stirring from their piles on the streets – gaunt women with babies strapped to their backs, old men being helped to their feet by children who looked no older than four or five. A boy ran up to her with outstretched hands.

She dug into her knapsack and retrieved an unopened sleeve of Ritz crackers, which she handed to the boy. Dessie had religiously supplied her with care packages ever since she'd left home for university and hadn't stopped when she'd come to Vietnam. The familiar treats, plus necessities like Tampax and medications, had been a lifeline for her, even though she prided herself on her ability to adapt to Southeast Asian life.

The orphanage was astir with activity when she arrived. A group of unfamiliar women – aid workers, the porter said – were busy at a table in the former dining room of the villa with piles of documents. Mel went first to check on Tien. The little girl was awake in her crib, staring solemnly at a patch of light that had been prismed by an angled window.

Mel lifted her up and murmured a few words in Vietnamese. There was no recognition in Tien's eyes and her body was stiff in Mel's arms. The child lacked so much in caring and affection. Mel had hopes that a loving adoptive family would fill the emptiness.

"Can you help with the porridge this morning?" Sister Agatha was at her elbow. At least they were trying to fill the children's bellies here. Mel followed the nun with Tien still in her arms to the orphanage refectory, set her in a high chair and began spooning soupy rice gruel into her eager mouth. Sister Agatha brought in more babies and they worked their way through the nursery, with Mel managing to get most of the food into the babies' mouths despite her fumbling. She was finishing up, wiping the remnants of the meal from the chin of the last baby, when two of the aid workers arrived in the refectory like women on a mission.

"There you are!" the older one blurted. She looked like a country club matron, with carefully coiffed blond hair and an outfit appropriate for shuffleboard on a cruise ship. The other one Mel sized up as ex-Army, all tightly buttoned up and rigid backbone compared to the flounce and pastel softness of the blonde. She had a clipboard in her hand and was wearing sensible shoes.

"Reverend Mother told us about you, and first of all, let me thank you for what you've done for the children. It's an honor to actually meet you!"

Mel wiped her sticky hands and put out her right one.

"Thank you. And you are . . .?"

"Oh, forgive me. I'm Pamela Boniface, and this is Trudy Parsons. We're volunteers from the Vietnamese Rescue League, here to organize the evacuation of the children. I just arrived in Saigon and Trudy's been on the ground for months. I'm the one who can pull the strings in Washington. Senator Smith and I go way back. His wife and I were college roommates and she's godmother to one of my sons. Anyway, it was the senator who got the President to authorize American military transport for us. After yesterday's tragedy, we need all the planes we can get, and we need to move quickly."

"Which is why we're coming to you," Trudy interrupted.

"I don't understand." Everyone seemed to think Mel had some direct line to power and the ability to work miracles.

"Now that we have the planes, we have to staff them, not just with a flight crew, but with adults who can accompany the children and care for them on the flights. We're putting the call out to any Americans within traveling range of Saigon. A contingent of Air Force nurses is coming from Hong Kong."

"And you want me to write a story about this?"

"Oh, no! We want you to fly with the children from St. Agnes."

Mel was stunned. It was the most ridiculous request that had ever been made of her.

"I'm not a nurse. Besides, my work is here in Saigon. I have no intention of leaving, especially not now."

Did these women not understand what was happening in the city? Did they think she wrote the news from a safe distance? She couldn't leave, not when one more story lurked amidst the chaos.

"I'm sorry. I'm not the person you need. I'm sure there are others here in Saigon who are desperately seeking to get out. The Embassy must have a lengthy list."

"Oh, my. This is a disappointment. Reverend Mother thought . . . Well, if you change your mind, we've got a plane for St. Agnes that will leave in a week. We're trying to get the paperwork processed for all the children. It's more problematic than I expected. The South Vietnamese government is not being as cooperative as I hoped."

"Now *that* is something I can be more helpful with. I know my way around the Vietnamese bureaucracy. Tell me what you need."

The disappointment expressed by Pamela was temporarily replaced with relief at Mel's offer. Mel followed the two women to the dining room to gather the list of missing documents.

"I still hope you'll reconsider, Miss Ames. Surely your family is anxious to see you."

Mel didn't respond. It hadn't mattered to her father that she'd been gone for so long, since most of the time he'd been away as well. But Mel knew how hard it was on Dessie. She'd been an incredible supporter, encouraging Mel to defy expectations throughout her upbringing, and had applauded Mel's accomplishments all along the way. But when Mel won this assignment to Saigon she had seen that Dessie had tried to hold her worry in check.

"You have to take risks in life if you are to truly understand what it means to live," she had preached to Mel whenever she had hesitated to do something she feared, or feared she might fail at. So Dessie had kept her mouth shut, hugged her hard at the departure gate the day she left and continued to send her care packages.

Mel took the list and headed off to the Ministry. She was glad to be doing something familiar – extracting information from officials – instead of juggling the needs of children who couldn't express themselves. She also didn't want to be at the orphanage when Phil arrived to do his rounds.

The fear and unrest mounting in the city had breached the barricades of the ministry. Confusion, resistance and anger greeted her wherever she went. Department heads barked at her, fists were slammed on tables, more forms in triplicate were thrust into her hands.

Realizing that the direct approach was not winning her the cooperation she needed, she retreated to the *Newsweek* office and began making phone calls. If ever there was a time to call in favors, this was it. She spent the next few days shuttling between ministries and on the phone, tracking down those who had the authority, or access to the authority, to grant the children the permission to leave.

She didn't stop as offices closed, but offered to meet her contacts in person at the Hotel Continental. She needed signatures, official stamps. If it meant a few hours in a smoky bar buying them expensive drinks, it wouldn't be the first time.

She had just wrapped up one of those meetings, her own drink barely touched as she had coaxed and flattered the self-important bureaucrat opposite her. But she had gotten what she wanted, thanked him profusely and sank into the worn banquette as she watched him swagger out the door. She took a quick sip of her drink and began gathering up her things to leave. Her head was down , stuffing her knapsack, when she heard the familiar voice.

"You're relentless, aren't you?"

"Excuse me?" She was caught off guard by Phil's presence. She'd managed to miss him at the orphanage, something her intellect had told her was a good thing. She'd been able to focus on what she needed to do for the children of St. Agnes rather than agonize about her conflicted reaction to spending the night at his flat. But her emotional need catapulted to the forefront as he stood on the other side of the table.

"I watched you from across the room. You weren't going to let him go until you got what you wanted. I wonder if he realized how well you played him."

"I was playing for keeps."

"I know. Reverend Mother told me you've taken on the entire South Vietnamese government to get the children released."

Mel noted the admiration in his voice and acknowledged to herself that she cared about what he thought of her.

"Mind if I join you while you finish your drink?"

"Oh, I was going to leave it...get going...a long day." She started to stand.

"Stay. Just a little while. I promise not to get on my soapbox about journalists."

She hesitated. Every moment she spent with him widened the chink in her armor, exposed more of her vulnerability. No one had seen her cry like Phil Coughlin. No one had held her like Phil Coughlin.

She sat down. *I'm going to regret this, in one way or another.*

"Why have you stayed in Saigon?" He looked around the nearly empty bar. Mel was the only woman.

"I could ask you the same question. Or rather, why did you come back?"

"You first."

"Because there is still a story to tell."

"And you told it. So why not leave now? Reverend Mother told me you refused a seat on the airlift."

"Reverend Mother appears to be telling you a lot of things about me. Is she trying to get you to convince me to fly with the babies?"

"No. She didn't volunteer any information about you. I had to pull it out of her. You don't like having the tables turned, do you? It makes you uncomfortable to have someone else asking the questions." He smiled.

She was startled by his curiosity about her. He was right, she was agitated—not because she found his questions intrusive, but because she found herself wanting to answer him. The heat she had felt simmering between them the morning after the crash—and the feelings she had managed to temper by avoiding him since then—now filled this desolate room. She took a gulp of her drink, staring into the sweating glass to avoid the intensity of his gaze.

"My turn. Why did you come back? I heard you left a job that would have set you up for life."

"A life I didn't want. My father, who *did* want it, blamed my decision on the Jesuits. I spent eight years being educated by them—high school and then Boston

College. Despite my best efforts to live up to my early reputation as a scruffy, troublemaking kid from the streets of South Boston, I seem to have absorbed the lessons of Ignatian spirituality that permeated everything we did at school."

"Ignatian spirituality?"

"The ideas developed by St. Ignatius Loyola, the founder of the Jesuits – basically, that we are on a continuous search for how best to live an authentic life. We were taught to ask where God will best be served and where people will best be helped."

"And the answer for you was not in Boston, but back here."

"Yes. When I recognized that, I had no choice but to come back. I was miserable and empty in Boston, just going through the motions."

"When I first met you, I thought that you were holding others to an impossibly high standard. Let me rephrase that. I thought that you were holding *me* to an impossibly high standard. But it's *yourself* that you demand so much of."

"You know, for someone who doesn't like me very much, you seem to have your finger on the pulse of who I am. There aren't many people who do."

Mel didn't deny that she disliked him. She'd never been able to camouflage what she truly thought of someone. But she was now recognizing that Phil's arrogance and party-boy reputation were barriers he had thrown up to mask a deeply felt compassion that an ex-Marine was not supposed to show. It was only when he was with the children—at St. Agnes and during the rescue—that he let down the mask. And the night he had comforted her in her nightmare.

"You're growing on me," she acknowledged. "Especially when you don't hide behind the perfect Phil Coughlin you present to the world."

"You're growing on me, too. I admit, I took you for a single-minded, hard-bitten journalist whose only interest in St. Agnes was to build your own reputation and pull some strings for the child of someone who had done you a favor. You've got your own mask protecting you. You're full of surprises, Melanie Ames. And I like what I'm discovering."

He lifted his glass to her.

"I guess that makes two of us." And she touched her glass to his.

Beyond the windows of the bar Melanie could see dusk falling; the tension in the city was rising and she didn't want to be out on the street after dark.

"I can give you a lift home," Phil offered, when he followed her gaze.

Mel didn't trust herself to accept. The conversation had already dissolved her resistance beyond the conflicted feelings that had haunted her as relentlessly as her nightmares. If she went with him, she wouldn't want to leave him. It was insane to open herself up to the possibilities taunting her in this complex and compelling man who had reached out to her across the divide between them. Saigon was about to fall. She had no idea where she'd be when it did, and she knew that wherever it was, there was no room for someone like Phil Coughlin. And she also knew that there was no room in Phil Coughlin's life for someone like her.

"I'd love to accept. But I need to make my own way home. Good-bye and thanks for…"

He stopped her, placing two fingers on her lips. "Not yet. Not good-bye. Not thank you."

As she left the room she watched him order another Scotch, remaining alone at their table.

Phil was right that it wasn't yet time for good-bye. They saw each other again at the orphanage, and Mel was relieved that, surrounded by the children and the heightened tempo of activity, the emotional charge between them was muffled. But she couldn't deny that she was acutely aware of the aura he spread throughout the villa even before she saw him. The children were more animated, dancing around him with gleeful smiles; the nuns, especially the younger ones, hovered near him, soaking up the energy field that seemed to surround him like the halo of a saint. Even Reverend Mother came under his spell, her austere demeanor somehow lightened, hopeful, by the reassurance he supplied, like the lollipop he pulled out of his pocket to hand to a child he'd just inoculated.

His presence was calming to Mel, as well. He possessed a sureness that what they were doing was right, and Mel began to understand what he meant by the spiritual force that had led him back to Saigon. She questioned whether she would ever know with such certainty that she was following the right path.

Phil sought her out after he finished what had brought him to the orphanage—delivering supplies for the flight that he had scrounged around the city, completing medical exams that were required before the children could leave, ministering to the gravely ill children who were still arriving at the doorstep. They were both exhausted, driven, acutely aware that they had little time left to save the children of St. Agnes. But they found a few moments to talk over a cigarette in the courtyard, Mel leaning back against the wall with her eyes closed and Phil crouched in the position he often took to bring himself down to the level of the children.

"What will you do when this is over?" Mel tried to tell herself that her reason for asking was simply the natural curiosity of the reporter.

"I'm not sure yet. I'll go wherever I'm needed. One doesn't have to look very far – perhaps just across the border in Cambodia. And you?"

"Wherever *Newsweek* sends me. The next war. There doesn't seem to be a shortage."

"Will you go home?"

Mel hadn't considered that question. She missed Dessie. But after three years in Saigon she felt completely detached from the life she had left behind in Georgetown.

"I don't know. I don't belong there anymore."

"I know what you mean. This place, this life, changes people irrevocably. One can't go back to who one was before." He put out the cigarette and rose. Both of them went back into the villa and the challenges confronting them within its walls.

The next day, the day before the flight was supposed to leave, Anh came to the orphanage for the last time to say goodbye to her daughter. Mel almost didn't recognize her in her *ao dai*. It was pale yellow, the silk dress skimming Anh's body over wide trousers. The traditional gown transformed her from tough, war-weary bar girl to elegant and stoically contained young woman. Her face was scrubbed of makeup and she had pulled her hair back into a chignon. Even the porter and the nuns noticed the difference.

Mel knew what it must have taken for Anh to make this last visit, reopening the wound caused by her decision to relinquish Tien to a future without her. She took her daughter from the nursery and sat alone with her on the verandah, rocking her silently for nearly an hour. No one disturbed them.

Elsewhere in the villa, Phil was busy organizing group photos of the children. He had arrived earlier with a camera, convincing Reverend Mother to gather the children to commemorate the final days of the orphanage. He offered to take a photo of Anh with Tien. She hesitated, then shyly agreed. Mel watched them – Anh solemnly staring at the camera; Tien curled into her mother's arms.

When Anh saw Mel, she waved her to her side.

"Take another one with us both, please," Anh said to Phil.

Up close, Mel could see the tears brimming in Anh's eyes. She put her arm around her and held her long after Phil had snapped the picture.

Later that night, she wearily climbed the stairs to her flat, her mission almost completed. She'd succeeded in getting the papers for all but ten of the St. Agnes children and had promises that she'd have the remaining documents the next day.

Inside the flat she found a note on the floor, apparently shoved under the door. It was in Mrs. Bao's hand.

"Grandmother call. Father ill. Come home."

Mel glanced at her watch. It was late morning in Washington. She couldn't tell from the note when Dessie had called. Mel's grandmother might be frantic with worry, especially when news like the plane crash heightened the perception in the States of just how dangerous the situation in Saigon was. It wasn't like Dessie to exaggerate, to create a reason to call Mel home unnecessarily. Dessie always told the truth, unembellished.

Despite the hour, Mel retraced her steps and knocked on Mrs. Bao's door, the note still in her hand.

"Missy, I wonder where you are all day. Not want to worry Grandma. But you must call."

Mrs. Bao opened the door wider and ushered Mel inside to use the phone.

The connection took longer than usual. Mel found herself tapping her fingers on the table, impatient and anxious. Questions raced through her brain. She needed information to quell the unease that the news of her father's illness had set in motion. Despite his absence from her life, Mel had always considered him indestructible, a survivor of violent encounters, a man who confronted and triumphed over wrongdoing. Illness was something she had never considered.

When she finally heard Dessie's voice on the line Mel sought the reassurance and solidity that her grandmother had always provided her. But for the first time it wasn't there.

"Oh, Melanie, thank God! I thought you might be out of reach, off on some assignment, and it would be too late."

"Too late? What do you mean, Grandma? What has happened to Daddy? Where is he?"

"He's had a massive heart attack, honey. He's at Walter Reed Hospital, and needs surgery. They're going to operate today. It's time for you to come home, Melanie. For *your* sake. Can you get a flight out? We can probably call someone at the State Department if there's a problem."

Dessie sounded frail and exhausted, but unwavering in her conviction that Mel should come home. Mel knew there had been times in the past when her father had been in danger – death threats, consulates under siege – and Dessie had protected her from the knowledge, not burdening her with fear. But she wasn't protecting her now.

For the second time in a week Mel began to cry, quiet tears slipping down her cheeks. She wiped them away and answered Dessie in as strong a voice as she could muster.

"I know of a flight that will take me tomorrow, Grandma. I'll be in San Diego by Sunday and grab a plane to D.C. from there. Don't worry. I'll make it home."

"Thank you, honey. I'll let your father know."

"Is he conscious?" she asked.

The phone crackled with static and the connection was broken. Mel replaced the receiver without learning the answer.

Mrs. Bao was waiting in the shadows, wringing her hands.

"Not good? You go now, not come back?"

Mel acknowledged that Mrs. Bao was right. Leaving on the flight to San Diego most certainly meant she would not be coming back.

Mrs. Bao, normally restrained and measured in her interactions, reached out and stroked Mel's tear-stained cheek.

"You good girl, Missy. Good to Grandma, good to Saigon, good to Bao family. Take care of family. Take care of self."

Mel closed her hand over Mrs. Bao's.

"Thank you. Take care of yourself, too, Mrs. Bao."

The next morning, her duffle bag packed and slung over her back, Mel stopped at the *Newsweek* office to leave word of her departure. Joe was there, fumbling with the coffee pot.

"Good luck, kid. Sorry to hear about your dad. Hope everything turns out okay. See you in the next war."

At the orphanage, the tension was unmistakable. Several more unfamiliar people were in the villa, conferring with Reverend Mother, furiously leafing through documents, making phone calls.

Mel waded through a maze of boxes and people to find Pamela Boniface. Her flowered blouse was a little rumpled this morning, but she was still meticulously groomed, her bright red fingernails rifling through a sheaf of documents.

"Pamela, I've reconsidered. If there is still room, I'll fly with the babies."

Pamela looked up in surprise.

"Oh, I knew we could count on you!" Mel had no intention of telling this woman why she had changed her mind. She opened up her knapsack and pulled out a stuffed brown folder bound with a rubber band.

"Here are all the stamped release forms I was able to get. My contact is working on the forms for the older boys that the government is holding up."

She spent the morning with Reverend Mother, Pamela, and Trudy reviewing the logistics: the buses that would carry the children to the airport; the boxes of supplies—diapers, formula, blankets—that had been gathered from around the city; the preparation of the final manifest.

Every hour some new piece of information was brought to their attention; plans were adjusted, expectations realigned. The pace of activity suited Mel. It didn't give her time to think about her father and what awaited her when she arrived back in the States. But it did not obscure the loss gnawing at the edges of her concentration. She had known for weeks that the time she had remaining in Saigon was limited and she had made her farewells to the few people who mattered to her. But with her unexpected departure now only hours away, she was acutely conscious of the one goodbye that remained unspoken.

"Do you expect Dr. Coughlin before we leave?" she asked Reverend Mother, trying to restrain the urgency she knew her voice must be conveying.

The nun looked at her, and realization spread across her lined face. "So his effect has reached you, as well. Oh, my dear girl, I should have guessed that two people so committed to saving our children would have found in one another a kindred soul."

Mel was about to deny such a profound connection, but acknowledged that the nun had spoken the truth. Her face crumpled in despair.

"Found, and lost in the same moment. Our lives are about to diverge. Who knows what lies ahead for either of us?"

The nun took her hands. "Life, especially in times like these, is filled with uncertainty. Trust that if it's meant to be, you'll find each other again."

Mel wanted to believe her, but the turmoil of the last twelve hours in her own life, coupled with the desperation surrounding her in the city, had taken its toll. Nothing seemed permanent or secure. The image of her father in a hospital bed tethered to machines and the prophetic nightmares of the last two weeks had crushed her childlike belief that her father would always be somewhere in the world, that Dessie would always be her rock and her comfort, that she herself had the resilience and strength to make her way no matter what befell her.

The fear that she had been reading on the faces of the refugees inundating the city was now lapping at her ankles. She felt it rising in her, threatening to drown her. She had never known herself to be so adrift. The clamor and frantic pace of the preparations around her heightened her shattered sense of control. She managed to whisper a thank-you to the nun and retreated to the courtyard, hoping to compose herself.

It was there that Phil found her.

"I heard that you were leaving with the children. Is it true?"

He seemed as unprepared as Mel for her departure. The anguish in his question laid bare what was still unspoken between them, what they no longer had the time to reveal to one another.

She nodded.

"Why the change of heart? I thought you planned on writing the last story of this war."

She hadn't meant to share with anyone the reason for her decision to leave, but in her vulnerable state the words came tumbling out, along with the self-doubt that she was neither as brave nor as strong as she had once imagined herself to be.

"I'm sorry about your father. But don't lose faith in yourself. We're all afraid, Melanie. But what I've seen in you since you first set foot in the villa convinces me that you'll prevail over your fears. Now, more than ever, the children need you to be strong. I know you won't fail them. You're an amazing woman. You have to know that you've saved the children of St. Agnes, not only with your talent, but also with your persistence."

He looked away from her and added, "And you've saved me."

"Saved you? From what?"

"From myself. One of the Jesuit tenets I never bothered to master was humility. I know I can be insufferably cocky and full of myself, buying into the humanitarian and healer labels the world has bestowed on me and convincing myself that because I was on a mission, anything I did to accomplish it was right. You stood up to my bullshit. You spoke the truth. Thank you."

"I'm the one who needs to say 'thank you.' You pushed me to see beyond myself."

"I wish we had more time. Just think of all the improvements we could effect in each other." He smiled, and she rewarded him with a smile of her own. It eased the intensity of their revelations and postponed for a few brief moments the reality that awaited them.

"Will you ride with us to Tan Son Nhut?"

"No. I'm leaving for Cambodia this evening. With the orphans being evacuated, my work here is done."

"Then this is where we say goodbye?" She couldn't hide the pain in her voice.

"Not goodbye. I told you that the other night at the Continental." He was gentle in his correction of her words.

"What do we say?"

"This," he said. And took her face in his hands, drew her toward him, and kissed her. His breath, his pulse, his courage, his compassion filled the emptiness that had been carved out by her fear. They held each other in silence until the afternoon rain began its steady drumbeat and the buses pulled into the courtyard.

The ride to Tan Son Nhut was wrenching. The familiar landmarks of the city rolled by the clouded windows of the bus. Many of the buildings were empty, abandoned by merchants who had been serving Americans for almost a decade but who had seen the handwriting on the wall. A Coca-Cola sign flapped in the steamy breeze hanging by one corner, a broken chain dangling from the other.

From the moment the buses entered the heavily guarded airport past a desperate throng pressed up against the chain link fence, Mel understood how challenging of a journey lay ahead of her. Tien began to cry as soon as they boarded the plane and could not be consoled. Improvising, Mel wrapped her in a sling and carried her for hours—first as they settled the children in their seats and makeshift cradles and then as an emigration official compared the information on the tag pinned to each child with the documents Mel had secured, his face impenetrable as he scrutinized every detail. She felt out of character balancing a baby on her hip. It was at once both unfamiliar and reinforcing. It was something so simple, but so clearly right for Tien, who responded with her body. She realized how incongruous she might look to her *Newsweek* colleagues, standing up to power and authority with a baby in her arms. But in a strange way she felt infused with a power all her own because of Tien. She was the fiercely protective she-wolf guarding her pups from predators. No one was going to take any of these children off the plane.

As soon as the official reluctantly signed off on the manifest, they were cleared for take off. Mel glanced out the window. Night had fallen. "Farewell, Saigon," Mel whispered. "Farewell, Phil." They lifted off and the plane banked toward the China Sea and the unknown.

The next twenty hours were a blur, caring for the children, snatching a few hours of rest and all the while holding Tien close to her.

When they landed in San Diego nurses and ambulances were waiting on the runway to whisk the children away to the base hospital for checkups and care.

Mel stood in the doorway of the plane, Tien asleep and still sprawled across her hip in the sling. She blinked in the brilliant California sunshine, her eyes adjusting from the dimness of the plane. Around her everyone was crisp and energetic and efficient. She descended the stairs and a pair of hands reached out to take Tien from her.

As the nurse slipped her out of the sling, Tien woke up, took one look at the strange face and began to scream.

"It's okay, sweetie. It's okay." She held the unhappy, struggling baby with practiced ease. "I'm a pediatric nurse and I go through this all the time with kids and their moms. She'll calm down soon," she reassured Mel.

"She hasn't been separated from me since we left Saigon. I'm not so sure she's able to calm down."

"Don't worry. It's frightening for all children to have their routines disrupted. But the good news is, they're flexible and, at this age, their memories are short. We'll get her cleaned up and fed and before you know it, she'll be united with her adoptive family and settling into life as a little American girl."

"She doesn't have a family yet. The agency hasn't identified one. Where will she stay?"

"Here on base for a few days. Then the agency responsible for her will take custody."

All the while, Tien continued screaming and reaching out for Mel.

"You need some rest. We've got temp quarters set up for you aid workers in the gym. Hot showers, hot meal, a real bed. Go ahead, take care of yourself now."

She pointed to a bus waiting to transport the adults.

Mel felt the accumulated fatigue and emotional assault of the last few weeks; she also felt an emptiness where she had carried Tien against her body.

She reached out for the little girl and took her back into her arms.

"I'll stay with her until I know she's settled down," she said and went with Tien to the hospital.

Mel was grateful for the continued efficiency of everyone at the base, although the sunny can-do attitudes grated somewhat against her darker view of humanity. Tien was quickly examined and cleared. Rather than risk another bout of inconsolable crying, Mel bathed and dressed her herself.

Someone even provided a rocking chair along with a warm bottle and the two of them drifted into a state of contentment that Mel hadn't known before. When Tien was finally in a deep sleep, a nurse showed Mel to a crib where she could lay her down. Mel hovered over her for several minutes, expecting another outburst, but she was clearly sound asleep and Mel tiptoed out of the room.

As she passed the nurses' station, the nurse on duty stopped her.

"Are you Melanie Ames, the reporter who arrived on the Babylift flight this afternoon?"

Mel groaned inwardly as she acknowledged who she was. What, had *Newsweek* already tracked her down, chomping at the bit for a story about the flight?

"We have a phone message for you, asking you to call someone named Dessie."

Mel's heart, already pulled in so many directions in the last 24 hours, plunged. She found the phone the nurse pointed her towards and hoped as she dialed with trembling fingers that Dessie had called only to reassure herself that Mel had arrived safely in San Diego.

Mel almost didn't recognize Dessie's voice when she answered the phone, it was so frail and distant. She sounded to Mel like she was under water and later Mel understood that it had been the water of her tears that had so distorted her speech.

"Grandma, it's Melanie. I've arrived safely in San Diego."

"Oh, sweetheart, thank God! I couldn't bear it if I lost you, as well."

"Lost me, as well? What do you mean, Grandma?" But she knew exactly what Dessie meant.

"Melanie, your father passed away this morning after surgery. His heart . . . just not strong enough . . . too damaged . . . nothing they could do to save him."

She seemed to be repeating a litany, unable to truly grasp the reality of her son's death. She began to cry.

Mel held her own tears in check to comfort her grandmother.

"Oh, Grandma. I'm so sorry. I'll be home as soon as I can get a flight out of here. We'll be together. We'll be all right."

"Yes, hurry home, honey. I need to put my arms around you."

"I will, Grandma. I'll be there soon."

Mel hung up the phone, stunned. She had somehow managed all during the flight to deny her reason for flying in the first place. She slid to the floor on her knees and leaned her head against the cool tile of the wall as her own tears finally began to flow.

It was the nurse who had given her the phone message from Dessie who found her. She handed her a box of tissues.

"I'm so sorry. When you're ready, I'll have someone come pick you up and get you over to the gym. You need some rest, probably some food. When was the last time you ate?"

The nurse helped her up and sat her in a chair by the nurses' station until she could catch her breath.

Another helpful soul ferried Mel across the base to the gym, where she stood under a hot shower for twenty minutes. There, mingled with her tears, the dust and memories of Saigon ran off her body and down the drain. She was crawling into a cot after picking at the roast beef dinner the base had provided, when a messenger came searching for her.

"Miss Ames? The hospital just called. The baby's been screaming for half an hour and nobody knows what to do for her. They're asking if you'll come back."

Mel swung her legs onto the floor and accompanied the messenger back to the hospital. She could hear Tien's wails from down the corridor, and her body responded as if she herself were in pain. She began to run down the hall, arriving breathless at the door to the nursery and throwing off whatever burdens of fatigue or need had plagued her earlier. In that moment, she understood that Tien had become a part of her. The aching loss that her father's death had precipitated had somehow been filled by the child who had clung to her since she left Saigon. The doubts that had swirled in her head during her last traumatic weeks in Vietnam were suddenly dispelled. She knew now what she was meant to do. She was meant to be Tien's mother.

She went to the little girl and enveloped her with arms that seemed to Mel to have grown in strength since she'd left Saigon.

"I'm here, baby. Mama's here. And I won't leave you again."

Part Two

THIRTY YEARS LATER

The ferry *Martha's Vineyard* eased out of its berth at Woods Hole on Cape Cod and turned toward the island after which it was named. Mel climbed the narrow metal stairs to the top deck and stood at the prow, the wind whipping her hair as gulls hovered overhead and a few early morning sailors tacked away from the shipping channel.

She could have flown from DC to the Vineyard – along with half the Massachusetts Congressional delegation – but in addition to not wanting to get stuck sitting next to a senator who would feel compelled to expound on the latest national crisis, she simply loved this early morning voyage across Nantucket Sound.

She had always driven her beat-up Subaru from Georgetown every summer when she came to stay with

Dessie at the cottage on Cape Pogue that had been in the family since before Mel was born.

When Tien had been a child all three of them had driven together – Mel at the wheel and Dessie in the back entertaining her great-granddaughter as they made their way up the congested I-95 corridor. When they arrived on the island they had opened the cottage for the summer, airing out rooms that had been sealed against winter storms, making beds, inspecting for weather damage or habitation by mice and squirrels. Mel enjoyed the industry of those first few days, rolling up her sleeves and attacking cobwebs and dust bunnies and mouse droppings. It was a far cry from the intellectual life she led as a reporter and columnist for *The Washington Post*.

Before Dessie had passed away last year at the age of ninety-six, she had asked Mel to promise her that she would go back to the cottage at least one more summer.

"Oh, Grandma! I wouldn't miss it. Cape Pogue is very special to me."

"I know, dear. That's why I don't want you to lose what I saw it giving you every summer. Not just a respite from work, but a replenishment of your soul. You've always been so hard on yourself, Melanie. Especially when you were young and felt you had so much to prove.

"I am certainly proud of all your accomplishments – not everyone at my women's club had a granddaughter who'd won not one, but *two* Pulitzer Prizes." Her eyes twinkled in amused recollection of her bragging rights even in the heady environment of Georgetown. "But more than anything, I want you to know that you are a wonderful mother."

When Mel had embraced Tien as her daughter she also made the decision to find work that would keep her close to home. She vowed not to abandon Tien for her job as her own father had her. Her reputation established by the work she'd done for *Newsweek*, it has been easier than she'd thought possible to secure a slot with the *Post*. She had expected the transition from war correspondent to a city beat at a metropolitan newspaper – even one in the nation's capital – to be confining. She had anticipated the dismissive attitudes of her male colleagues in Saigon, who were heading off to the next conflagration without her to make their coffee or do their research. But she hadn't known that the choices she made by Tien's crib in San Diego – to adopt Tien and stay home to raise her – would ultimately be so satisfying. Mel had no regrets.

Tien had developed into an extraordinary young woman, flourishing as a high school teacher in a challenging school in the Bronx after graduating from Mel's alma mater, Columbia. Most summers Mel stopped in New York to pick her up on the way to Woods Hole, but this year Tien was making her way separately, flying in from Wisconsin, where she'd been working as a counselor at a camp for Vietnamese children who'd been adopted by American families. She'd gone there herself as a teenager, one of the attempts Mel had made to help Tien understand her own heritage.

The loudspeaker advising drivers to return to their vehicles broke Mel's reverie on the deck and she headed below to join the line of escaping vehicles as the ferry pulled into the harbor at Oak Bluffs. Even at eight in the morning the dockside was bustling, and Mel maneuvered through SUVs towing boat trailers and mounted with bicycle racks until she was on Barnes Road and headed for the airport.

Tien had caught a Cape Air flight out of Boston after traveling the day before from Milwaukee, so she was exhausted and more subdued than her usual chatty self. Mel knew that Tien loved coming to the Vineyard as much as she did and chalked up her daughter's withdrawn demeanor to fatigue. A nap in the hammock on the lawn overlooking the pond, a meal of freshly dug clams and a glass of wine on the porch as the sun set this evening would revive her.

It was the first time either of them had been to Cape Pogue without Dessie. Jerry Soames, the handyman on the island who cared for the place in the off-season, had already removed the boards that protected the windows during winter storms and had made sure the propane tanks were full. The cottage had no electricity and everything – the stove, refrigerator, gas lamps and water heater – ran on propane. Jerry had even raised the flag on the pole outside the house. Glancing down the beach

Mel could see flags snapping in the breeze in front of other cottages. It was a common practice among the few families who inhabited this isolated stretch of land on the northern tip of Chappaquiddick – their sign to neighbors that they were there.

Mel and Tien quickly dispatched the preliminaries of settling into the achingly familiar place and then Mel shooed Tien off to sleep. While Tien retreated to the cozy bedroom she'd always used, Mel took a deep breath and opened the door to Dessie's room.

It reflected Dessie's touches: a white iron bedstead, a quilted coverlet faded to pale blues and greens, a bundle of dried lavender hanging above the bed reawakening Mel's memory of her grandmother's scent. On a table next to the bed was a wooden box Mel had never seen before.

When Tien woke from her nap Mel was still in the bedroom, the contents of the box strewn across the bed around her.

"What's all this?"

"Mementos Gigi had apparently saved of the times the family spent here."

"Gigi" had been Tien's name for Dessie, short for great-grandmother.

Tien joined her on the bed to look at the photos and notes. She picked up one of a smiling young woman in a sundress holding a little girl by the flagpole.

"Who are they?"

"That's me with my mother."

"Do you remember her?"

"Yes. I especially remember spending summers here with her and my grandparents while my father was away."

Tien stroked the photo thoughtfully. Mel watched a look of longing cross her daughter's face and was puzzled by Tien's reaction to the photo.

"You're lucky to remember her. There's so much family history here," Tien mused, as she glanced at the array of pictures spanning almost fifty years.

"Look, here's you and me in almost the same pose," Mel said. "Gigi must have remembered the older photo and had us recreate it."

Later in the day the two women walked along the beach, empty except for a couple of fly fisherman hoping to catch a few blues.

Their walk was a ritual for them every year when they came to the island, an opportunity to catch up with each other since they'd seen each other last.

Mel remembered the first time Tien had returned from the Wisconsin camp at the age of eight, armed with recipes and a vocabulary list. When Mel had first adopted her she gave her the American name of Christine, a common practice among the families adopting the Babylift children. But in addition to the foods and language she'd been introduced to at camp, Tien had also learned the meaning of her Vietnamese name – fairy or spirit – and wanted to reclaim it.

"My name is Tien," she had corrected Mel and Dessie several times. "I want to be called Tien." So Tien she became.

As they walked, arms linked, along the water's edge, Mel sensed that once again her experience at the Vietnamese camp had triggered some transformation in Tien. She no longer assumed that it was merely jet lag and sleep deprivation that had silenced her daughter. Something was on her mind that she was finding difficult to share with her mother.

"You've been very thoughtful since you arrived. Anything you want to talk about?"

Mel felt Tien stiffen and turn to look out over the horizon. An osprey swooped overhead returning with food to its nestlings.

"I'm not sure where to begin. It's something that's been on my mind for a long time. I just haven't felt compelled to act until now. Being at the camp and then, this afternoon, sifting through all those photographs of your family, I realized it's always going to gnaw at me."

Mel did not miss that Tien had said *your* family, not *our* family.

Tien stopped walking and faced Mel, her hands at her side.

"I need to find Anh. I want to know my Vietnamese family."

Mel saw the longing in her daughter's eyes. She also saw her searching Mel's eyes for approval and acceptance. Mel put her arms around Tien.

"Oh, honey, of course you do!"

"It's okay with you?" Tien's voice was flooded with relief.

"Sweetheart, I know what it means to want to know who your mother is. There were so many times in my life when I wished and longed for mine."

"I don't even know where to begin."

"I can help you. I'm an investigative reporter, remember!"

For the next two weeks, while soaking up the peace and serenity that Pogue always brought her, Mel began what she could of the search to reunite Tien with Anh. A trip to the library in Edgartown to use the computer gave her some of the information she needed; a phone call provided a few leads.

Mel was going through the motions, doing everything she could think of to support Tien – from that first embrace to reassure her on the beach to hunting down contacts who might still have knowledge of the orphanage.

But late at night alone in her bed, Mel feared that every step she was taking to help Tien was also placing one more step between them. Despite her intellectual grasp that bringing Tien closer to Anh was not a zero-sum game – her actions weren't taking Tien away from her – emotionally she felt at risk of losing her daughter.

The night before they left the island, they sat at the dining room table with Mel's notes. She had accumulated enough information and developed a list of contacts that it made sense for Tien to go to Vietnam and continue in person to seek Anh. Tien was excited, but also distressed.

"I don't think I can do this on my own. I'm a schoolteacher who's used to lesson plans and curricula and established criteria. I like knowing what to expect. I'm not sure I can deal with the uncertainty and ambiguity. I don't want to do this alone."

Mel looked across the table. Instead of the competent grown woman she knew her daughter to be, she saw the frightened little girl who had clung to her on the flight from Saigon.

She knew she would pick her up and carry her this time. as well.

"Shall I come with you?" she asked quietly.

"Would you? Thank you, Mom!"

In the next few weeks, they made preparations for the trip. Mel took a leave of absence from the newspaper with her editor's blessing – she suspected because he anticipated she might be persuaded to write a story about Tien's quest for her mother. Mel's writing was deeply personal and often tapped into her own experience; but she had always drawn the line when it came to Tien's life. Raising a daughter had been challenging enough without having to deal with her feeling that her mother had told her secrets to the world. Tien was no longer a teenager, but this journey was as emotionally draining as adolescence.

Mel also acknowledged to herself that returning to Vietnam awakened feelings she thought she had long put to rest. Although Phil Coughlin had disappeared into the killing fields of Cambodia after Saigon fell, he had not disappeared from her heart. What might life have held for them if they had been able to fulfill the promise of those last few days in Saigon? As she had been when she was in her twenties, Mel wasn't one to dwell on loss. But in anticipating this journey she found herself tinged with regret that they had let slip from their hands something she knew now had been precious and irredeemable. With her usual practicality, she brushed aside these flickers of distraction. She had work to do.

Before she knew it, she and Tien had their visas and tickets, letters of introduction to the ministries that might have records, and a short list of contacts to start their search.

The night before they were to leave, Tien took the Acela from Penn Station in New York to D.C. Normally composed and self-contained, she spent the evening at Mel's pacing, repacking and questioning every aspect of their plans.

"Do you think the gifts I've gotten are appropriate? How do I know what she'll like?"

"Tien, let's find her first. And the best gift will be you – a beautiful, happy woman who cared enough about her to seek her."

"Am I being selfish? What if she doesn't want to be found?"

"Then we won't violate that wish. There are no guarantees here, Tien. Let's try to get some sleep. We have a long journey ahead of us."

As the plane descended into Tan Son Nhat International Airport, Mel found herself with her face pressed against the window, searching for the familiar. She didn't know what she was looking for – and after thirty years of postwar reconstruction, it was doubtful that she'd recognize it. But with a jolt she understood that this trip was as much a homecoming for her as for Tien. Even to be landing at Tan Son Nhat, and the incongruity of it now being an international airport and major hub for Vietnamese flights, seemed unbelievable.

The terminal was a chaotic mess of tourists scrambling to check in and find their gates. They'd arrived smack in the middle of monsoon season, and delays flickered across the departures and arrivals board. Tien seemed almost paralyzed by the assault on her senses, staring at the waves of people pushing past her, trying to decipher the lettering on the signs with her limited command of the language, unable to focus on any one thing as they moved through the airport. Her only comment to Mel was a revelation.

"They look like me. All of them. I'm not different here."

Mel should have grasped a long time ago what it had meant to her daughter to look out at the world and not see herself reflected in the faces looking back at her. Even if this trip did not result in their finding Anh, Mel understood even in these first few moments that what they learned – about themselves, about each other – would be immense.

They emerged from the terminal into oppressive heat and a curtain of rain. Mel had forgotten how aware one always was of the weather in Vietnam; she wondered if she was experiencing her first hot flash as they waited for the bus that would take them into the center of Ho Chi Minh City. With sweat dribbling down her armpits, she and Tien maneuvered their suitcases onto the bus and settled into two of the open seats. Mel had chosen the bus to bring Tien as close as possible to the life Mel remembered being lived on the streets of Saigon. The cocoon of a taxi or limousine sealed one away from everything there was to absorb in a city. With a map open on her lap, Mel pointed out landmarks, but what she saw passing by the windows of the bus resembled nothing that she remembered from the last bus ride she had taken on these same streets.

This was no longer "her" Saigon. The tawdriness, the sense of impending disaster, the frisson of danger that electrified every encounter, the mud, were all missing. In its place was a scrubbed and orderly city, new buildings, parks in which families strolled rather than sought refuge from the enemy to the north. Here and there she saw an older building, its façade still pockmarked. As the bus crossed Dong Khoi Street, she caught a glimpse of neon and saw that the bar district had not disappeared, only switched its clientele. She might find one or two of her familiar haunts and be able to say to Tien, "This is where Anh worked and where she asked me to help her get you out of the country."

They settled into their hotel and Mel asked at the desk for the closest noodle bar. The hotel staff tried to steer her toward Western-style restaurants, thinking they were a pair of neophyte American tourists. But Mel dragged up her rusty Vietnamese and convinced them she didn't need coddling, just good information.

They ate, returned to the hotel to sleep, and began their search in earnest the next morning. As they trekked from one ministry to another and made contact with each name on Mel's list, they felt themselves weaving a web. Their expectations were high as possibilities started to open up for them – the location of Anh's village; the name of a cousin.

A setback occurred three days into their search when they discovered that the villa that had housed St. Agnes had been destroyed as a vestige of the colonial era. No one knew what had become of the nuns. The news distressed Mel more than she expected. She'd not always understood the women who had run St. Agnes with such discipline and efficiency in the face of devastating deprivations; but to have even the memory of their existence wiped away as thoroughly as the building was to her incomprehensible and chilling.

Other fragments of her own history were missing as well – the Baos' tea house and the whole cluster of alleys where her flat had been located seemed to have been replaced by a block of modern apartments. She was disoriented by the transformation of the city and missed its seediness and dark corners.

On the fourth night they ventured to the bar district. As Mel had noted on the bus ride, it was still in the same place, throbbing with Japanese techno music and black lights. They wandered up and down the main avenue as Mel got her bearings, but as they rounded a corner a doorway hung with beads jogged her memory.

"That's it! That's the club where Anh worked." She steered Tien across the street and parted the curtain of beads. Inside was thronged with tourists – Chinese from Hong Kong, Australians, even some Germans from the conversations Mel was overhearing as they pushed further inside. The dance floor where Anh had entertained American soldiers was pulsating with young people while a DJ moved through his repertoire. The air was thick with cigarette smoke, knock-off perfumes, and rum. Mel, for the first time since arriving in the city, felt the prickle of familiarity. She saw herself at twenty in the bodies on the dance floor, the barely contained seductions, the excitement of the unknown unfolding itself in the rhythm of the music and the sweet taste of umbrellaed drinks.

Tien, on the other hand, drew back. Mel saw the discomfort in her daughter's eyes. Perhaps this was not how she had imagined Anh's life. Beneath the energy on the dance floor she was seeing the spilled drinks, the furtive groping.

"What do you expect to find here?" Tien shouted to Mel, trying to be heard above the pounding music, her face in the flashing lights pained. "No one will remember her. The bar girls are younger than I am."

But Mel wasn't thinking about asking the waitresses. Instead, she made her way to the bar where an older woman was mixing drinks. Tien followed reluctantly. Mel managed to eke out a few questions between record changes. The woman had only been working at the club for a few years; she'd come from Hanoi after the war. But she knew of one or two women who had worked here before; she took Mel's cell phone number and offered to pass it on to them.

Mel would have lingered, soaking up this one sliver of her history here, but Tien so clearly wanted to leave that she reluctantly led her back out onto the street.

"I just want to go back to the hotel and shower," she said, as if to cleanse herself of any connection to that place so irrevocably tied to her mother.

Tien's discomfort with Ho Chi Minh City – what it had been for Anh and Mel, what it was now – grew stronger over the next several days. The food was spicier than she liked and upset her stomach; she struggled to use her limited Vietnamese.

"Why didn't you insist that I learn Vietnamese when I was a child? All I can speak or understand are the baby phrases you used to say to me. How will I be able to communicate with my mother when we find her?"

Mel noticed that Tien was referring to Anh now not by name but as my *mother*.

The conversation with the woman in the club set off a series of connections as Mel's phone number apparently was being passed from one possible source to another. They went on a round of meetings with women who claimed to know Anh or know of her. Then a man called, a lawyer who had developed a specialty in helping the children of the Babylift find their families. He offered his services for a retainer.

Mel cautioned against trusting him, but Tien insisted on meeting him.

"We've turned up nothing so far. If he's been doing this as long as he says, he may have connections and access to records that we don't know about. At least hear him out!"

Mel acquiesced and accompanied Tien to the lawyer's office in a nondescript building, but only to protect Tien from what she suspected was an unscrupulous predator. When he pressed them for an advance payment before he began helping them, Mel refused.

"I need to see some evidence of your ability to assist us – some assurance that you can make the connections you claim," Mel said.

They jockeyed back and forth, neither speaking the other's language well, but understanding enough to get the message across. Mel did not budge, and ultimately the lawyer threw up his hands. "Then I cannot help you."

When they left the office, Tien was furious.

"You treated me like a child in there!"

"You told me yourself that you feel unsure speaking Vietnamese. I was only trying to make sure he understood."

"But why didn't you want to pay him? What if we've lost our only opportunity to find her?"

"I wanted him to see that he wasn't dealing with someone he could easily exploit. I don't trust him."

"You think I can't handle this on my own!"

"Tien, you asked me to help you. I'm trying to do that. I'm also trying to protect you against false hope."

"But you keep throwing obstacles in the way. You doubt *everyone*. I think you honestly don't want me to find my mother!"

"Tien, I promise you that I will persevere for you until we've exhausted every option, explored every possible shred of evidence. But you're hovering on the edge of obsession if you're willing to believe that some snake oil salesman can magically make Anh appear.

"I know these last two weeks have been frustrating, and so much less than you hoped. But don't let your need to find Anh turn into desperation. That will only make you easy prey for someone like him to take advantage of."

"Stop patronizing me! How can you possibly understand my need? You *know* who your family is. You *know* whose blood runs through your veins."

"*You* are my family, Tien," she whispered, crushed that her daughter did not understand the bond that had been forged between them.

They had been arguing in front of the lawyer's office. Mel believed that if she stayed there any longer they would both descend into a spiral of accusations about mothering and daughtering from which they might not recover.

"I need to be alone for awhile. I'll hail you a cab to take you back to the hotel and meet you there in a few hours," Mel said.

"I can do that myself."

"Fine." Mel turned toward the center of the city and began walking. Out of the corner of her eye she saw Tien go back into the lawyer's building, but she resisted the impulse to stop her and walked on.

She was angry – with Tien for not recognizing how vulnerable she was, with herself for her own ambivalence. Was Tien right, that she didn't truly want her to find Anh? She longed to offer Tien wisdom and reassurance. Instead, she fumbled as awkwardly as she had decades before when she had first held Tien in her arms.

She continued to walk, futilely seeking refuge in a city that was no longer hers. The closer she got to the center the more chaotic and alien it seemed. Horns blared. Motorbikes wove recklessly through a sea of three-wheeled trucks, pedestrians and bicycles. Heat simmered above the payment.

She felt oppressed – by the weather, by Tien's criticism, by her own weaknesses. She had a fleeting longing for the cigarettes she had given up when she became a mother. She could use something right now to distract her as she strode through the city, putting distance between herself and her daughter, between the past and the present. She doubted that a cigarette would do the trick, but decided she'd settle for some air conditioning and a long, cool drink. The afternoon rain had begun. Her sandals were soaked and starting to chafe, and her bare legs were splashed with mud.

She'd led herself to a neighborhood that held pockets of familiarity and realized she wasn't far from the old *Newsweek* office in the Hotel Continental. As she rounded a corner, she saw it up ahead. The hotel had been renovated rather than demolished. With relief, she rotated through the revolving door, shook out her umbrella and cast about for the bar, where she was happy to sink into one of the padded booths.

She ordered a tonic and lime and scanned the room. The place definitely appealed to a western tourist clientele.

Copies of the *Financial Times* and *Herald Tribune* were scattered about.

She was leafing through the *Herald* absentmindedly, refreshed by the drink and lulled by the monotony of falling rain, when her eye fell on a familiar face staring out from page three.

Phil Coughlin, even in a low-resolution black-and-white photo, bristled with energy and a penetrating brilliance. It stunned her, especially when he had been so recently in her thoughts. She read on, hoping that the article would divert her enough from the unsettling tension with Tien.

The MacArthur Foundation had just announced its latest round of Fellows and Coughlin was one of them. They referred to him as the "Mountain Doctor" for his work among the hill tribes of northern Thailand. It appeared that he had never left Southeast Asia. After he had crossed into Cambodia, ministering to the victims of Pol Pot, he'd made his way north, building clinics in the remote territory above Chiang Mai in Thailand. The facts of his achievements as a humanitarian were spare – a list of dates and deeds that was long but lifeless. He had apparently impressed the award committee, but Mel had no sense of who Phil Coughlin was now beyond the label that had been attached to him.

She folded up the paper and was about to leave when her phone rang. She assumed it was Tien and flipped it open, but the number was a Washington area code.

"Mel, this is Sam."

The feature editor at the *Post*. It was 2 a.m. in Washington.

"I'm sorry to bother you on your vacation, but Susan told me where you are, and, well, I need you to take an assignment."

"Sam, I'm on leave taking care of family business." *And messing it up.*

"I know. But hear me out first, please. The MacArthur Foundation just named a new set of Fellows and they are a quirky bunch, so we want to do an in-depth piece on them. It seems that one of them is in Thailand. You're closer than anyone I've got in the newsroom, and I understand that this guy rarely comes back to the States. He's something of a one-man Doctors Without Borders, a cowboy, from what little I could find about him. But he's willing to do an interview – maybe only because MacArthur told him he had to. I can fly you up there and back to Vietnam – 36 hours tops. Will you do it?"

Mel had enough stature at the paper to refuse, but she didn't immediately turn Sam down. She felt a duty to Tien to see this quest through to one answer or another, but the frustrations and hostility of the morning had left her questioning whether she was helping or hindering her daughter. She also was pulled in two directions by the subject of Sam's assignment. The flatness of the MacArthur press release had left her curious about what had shaped and driven Phil to a life so different from hers. But at the same time, she was wary of opening herself up—to her own regrets, to his judgment of the path she had chosen, even to why he had disappeared so thoroughly, never once trying to reconnect.

She drummed her fingers on the glass-topped table.

"Sam, let me think about it. I'll call you in a few hours."

She hailed a cab back to her own hotel, surprised by the discomfort Sam's request had triggered. She was a professional. A simple assignment like this – a profile of an accomplished man – was hardly challenging.

Sam was right; she could knock this off in a day or two. And the fear she had of getting drawn back into the vortex of emotion that Phil Coughlin had elicited in her so long ago seemed ridiculous. She had been young and inexperienced then, and more vulnerable than she had admitted to herself, caught up in the raw and desperate situation in Saigon.

She'd lived through a lot since those tumultuous days – raised a child; excelled in her profession; even been in and out of love a few times, although never married. She wasn't one to fall under anyone's charismatic spell now, no matter how piercing his blue eyes or engaging his smile or noble his mission.

Mel let herself into her hotel room. Through the open French doors she saw Tien sitting on the balcony and went out to join her. Although the rain had subsided, the air was still heavy and the balcony offered no relief from the sweltering heat.

Tien's face was taut and clouded with anger as she turned to Mel.

"Where have you been? I was worried."

Mel didn't answer her question. "Why didn't you call? I had my phone on."

"You seemed to want to be alone when you left me at the lawyer's office." Tien's voice was icy, accusatory.

"I thought we both needed time away from each other. How did you spend the rest of the day?"

"I met with someone. Mr. Nguyen made the arrangement. She was the right age, came from the same region. But she couldn't answer the questions you gave m e."

Mel had prepared a short list of questions that only Anh would be able to answer.

Mel read the disappointment and frustration in her daughter's eyes. She refrained from asking Tien how much she had paid for this hastily arranged and failed assignation. She knew Tien didn't need to hear an "I told you so." But she was also wary of the barely camouflaged anger just below the surface of Tien's remarks. It was clear to Mel that Tien was gathering up all the false leads and dashed hopes into a bundle that she was laying at Mel's feet. She could hear the unspoken litany – if only Mel had made an attempt to maintain contact with Anh after she and Tien left Vietnam; if only Mel had recognized that Tien would want – *need* – to know her mother and had begun the search when Tien was younger and leads were still fresh. Mel saw it dawning on Tien that she had begun too late, that she might not find Anh, and that it was all Mel's fault.

Mel, weary and unwilling to engage Tien in another verbal battle, decided to retreat into work. She told Tien about the call from Sam.

"So I'm going to fly up to Chiang Mai and do the interview. You're welcome to come with me if you want to, or you can stay here and continue the search – maybe you should go to Anh's old village."

"I'll stay. If word is starting to circulate among people who might have known her, I want to stick around – not be on some inaccessible mountain. Who knows if you'll even have cell reception?"

"Do you want me to arrange for an interpreter while I'm gone?"

"Mr. Nguyen has already taken care of that."

"I hope this avenue works for you, honey." And with that Mel got up, went into the bedroom, and called Sam to let him know she'd take the assignment.

By the next morning she had a round-trip ticket to Chiang Mai and a reservation for a four-wheel drive vehicle to get her up into the mountains to Phil Coughlin's compound. She felt both relief to be away from Tien's bitterness and an apprehension that she was heading into emotional territory that might be just as entangled.

As the plane landed in Thailand, she reminded herself that this upcoming interview was about Phil Coughlin and what compelled him to do extraordinary things, not what he thought about Mel Ames. Nevertheless, she steeled herself for an unsettling reunion.

Armed with the information Sam had emailed her and a map from the car rental agency, Mel navigated out of Chiang Mai and followed the highway towards the mountains. Sam had offered to get her a driver, but she'd always preferred being on her own. She wanted time to think, not have to banter in pleasantries with an eager-to-please chauffeur. She wasn't a tourist in need of pampering.

Although it was monsoon season here in northern Thailand, as well, the rain only lasted for an hour or so during the day and then brilliant sunshine burst onto the refreshed countryside. As the road became narrower and more serpentine, Mel discovered a breathtakingly beautiful landscape around each bend. But as she passed through tiny villages scattered up the mountain she also saw heartbreaking poverty.

It was mid-afternoon when she reached the intricately carved gate to the clinic compound. Her arrival was noticed first by a group of boys arrayed in an odd assortment of American t-shirts. "Minnesota Vikings," "Six Flags Atlanta," and "NPR" were scattered around a dusty pitch playing soccer as she rolled to a stop just inside the walls and parked next to a rusting Toyota pickup.

The boys clustered around her as she emerged from the car, chattering in a dialect that she assumed must be Lahu, the hill tribe in this region. She spoke Phil's name and one of the younger boys ran off to a large thatched bamboo building resting on stilts. As she listened to the boys she glanced around, taking in her surroundings and cataloguing them for later inclusion in her article. Several stilted buildings rimmed the courtyard, simple but well maintained. She remembered how orderly Phil's flat had been in Saigon and saw that same precision reflected on a much larger scale here. The entire compound bustled with activity – women shepherding small children, awaiting their turn at what appeared to be the main clinic; men unloading supplies from a flatbed truck; an older woman tending a vegetable garden.

A tall, thin man, his face lined from years witnessing the pain and suffering human beings inflicted upon one another, descended the stairs of one of the houses and crossed the courtyard toward her. As he approached she realized with barely contained surprise that it was Phil. He stretched out his hand and greeted her, but with wariness and discomfort.

"Po told me a round-eyed woman with hair like a boy had spoken my name. I assumed it was either a desperately lost tourist or the reporter from *The Washington Post* the Foundation had warned me to expect. They didn't tell me it would be Melanie Ames."

At least he recognized her, but beyond remembering her name, he seemed both distrustful and unwilling to acknowledge their shared history. She wondered what had so damaged him in the intervening years.

"They said they had pulled you away from your vacation. I apologize for the disruption. If I'd had any say in this, you'd still be sitting on a beach drinking mai tais and I'd be left alone to do my good works, of which the foundation seems so enamored. However, it appears that neither one of us had the option of refusing, so here you are. Welcome."

She wanted him to know that she could have refused but had chosen instead to come. But he seemed to think that she was like any other journalist sent to irritate him. In the face of that indifference, her own apprehensiveness about falling once again within his sphere seemed foolish and self-absorbed.

"Thanks for agreeing to meet with me," she answered, determined to tamp down the churning in her gut and silence the voice that was asking plaintively, "How can you not care that it is *me* who has come to do this story?"

She followed Phil around the compound, notebook in hand, observing, questioning, showing suitable appreciation for the ingenuity of the Lahu tribesmen who'd been able to create a medical village with the most meager of resources.

Phil was comfortable expounding on the services he and his small staff of rotating medical workers were able to provide to one of the most impoverished of the hill tribes. He was willing to talk about the mobile clinic he brought to the more remote tribes at higher altitudes. He even described a plan he had for trying to prevent the younger generation from developing the opium addiction that was widespread among the elders of the tribe.

But he remained opaque and resistant whenever Mel tried to steer the conversation to Phil himself – what had been the journey that ultimately brought him to these lush mountains? What about the hill tribes had so captured him that he would devote his life to them? He offered nothing that she could not see herself, presenting only the façade of the hero doctor, a self-aware and hardened version of the cocky bravado she remembered from decades before.

After little more than an hour, he was ready to dismiss her.

"I have the evening clinic to prepare for. Many of the Lahu men offer themselves out as labor in other villages and return late in the day. That's when I treat them. I can ask the cook to prepare you some tea before you go. Feel free to enjoy it on my veranda." He pointed up to the porch above them, jutting out on stilts. "The view is spectacular."

Mel, frustrated by her inability to elicit anything of the man's spirit and irritated by his abrupt dismissal and unwillingness to even sip a cup of tea with her, decided to leave without accepting his offer. Her phone rang.

"Excuse me, but it's my daughter. I must answer this." She turned and took a few steps away from him.

"Mom, oh, thank God you've got reception up there!" Tien sounded tightly wound, as if she wanted to leap out of the phone, grab Mel, and pull her back.

"Tien! What is it?" The distance she had felt between them in the last few days evaporated. She was once again a mother responding to a cry of need from her child.

"I think I've found her! This isn't some scam artist passed off on me by that lawyer. Someone in the Ministry of Child Welfare called this afternoon. They gave me an address and assured me that this was the Anh Tran who had relinquished the infant Tien Tran in 1975."

"Have you tried to contact her?"

"I only have an address, and I can't find a phone number in the directory. I'm going to have to go myself . . . but that's why I called." She was silent for a moment. The bitterness and frustration were gone from her voice.

"Mom, I'm sorry I was so angry with you the other day. I said things I shouldn't have. And you were right about Nguyen. He was only trying to take advantage of my need."

"I understand, sweetheart. All is forgiven."

"Mom, I don't want to go to her alone. Will you come back and be with me?"

"Of course I will. I've got a flight out of Chiang Mai in the morning. There is nothing to keep me here any longer."

Mel clicked the phone off and absorbed what she had heard from Tien. Although there were no certainties, this latest information about Anh was probably as good as they could get, given its source. Mel was excited for Tien. She had heard the anticipation in her voice – the hope – and she shared that with her. But at the same time, she was hit with the old fear that she was about to lose something very precious.

"Is something wrong?" Phil's voice broke her train of thought. "You look like you've been given devastating news."

Mel was exhausted and drained. She'd already regretted making the grueling trip, a waste of time for both of them given the paltry, sterile information she'd managed to obtain. She was angry with him – for his arrogance, for his lack of understanding of what she could have done for him with her story, for his unwillingness to acknowledge that something – however tenuous – had once existed between them.

She should have just shrugged off his question, refused the tea, and climbed into her car.

But she didn't.

Something seized her, perhaps ignited by the tentative reconciliation she'd just experienced with Tien on the phone and her own recognition that, as much as Phil had erected a wall between them, she'd allowed it to remain and had not even attempted to establish a connection with him. She'd played the objective, disinterested journalist instead of the woman whose life he had touched in an irrevocable way. Damn it, she was Mel Ames! Where was the fervor, the willingness to leap into unknown territory?

"I'll take that cup of tea you offered, but only if you'll join me and allow me to tell you what that phone call was all about."

She was about to make that leap and see if Phil Coughlin would follow her.

He shrugged and looked at his watch.

"I imagine I can spare a half hour."

He led the way up to the veranda and made the tea himself.

The view was indeed extraordinary, extending across the mountains to the west. Mel settled into a cushioned wicker chair and cradled the cup in her hands. With a jolt of recognition she saw it was one of the Red Sox mugs he'd had in Saigon.

"You still have these mugs!"

"I still have many things from Saigon. So you have a daughter. When did you marry?"

"I didn't. I adopted Tien."

"Tien?"

"The baby from St. Agnes I originally came to help before you persuaded me to rescue all of them."

"I had no idea." Phil seemed truly stunned, as if he had not imagined her ever considering such an action. "I didn't realize you intended to adopt her yourself."

"I didn't – intend to, that is. But by the time we arrived in San Diego, she had made it very clear what she intended – she wanted no one else but me."

"So she's a grown woman now. But clearly close to you, and upset about something that has upset you, as well."

"Was it that obvious?"

"When you ended the conversation, some realization affected you. I could see the change in your face. When you were talking with her, your tone and your expression were totally empathic. You were a mother with a hurting child. But after you got off the phone, it was *you* who was hurting."

It was Mel's turn to be stunned. For someone who had barricaded himself from her an hour before, he had nevertheless been tuned in to what she was experiencing. She swallowed another sip of tea and realized this was the opportunity she had been hoping for – the breach in the wall. She plunged in, willing to open herself up to him in the hope that he would reciprocate.

"Tien is in Ho Chi Minh City, where we've been for three weeks. Not on a beach." She looked up at him. I'm not some dilettante tourist soaking up local color, she wanted to say to him.

"We've been searching for Anh, the bar girl who was my friend and Tien's mother."

"Any progress?"

"Not until today. But the frustration of the search and my own ambivalence about finding Anh had pushed us to the edge a few days ago. The mother-daughter dance is a complicated one. The rhythm keeps changing and the steps get more intricate as you move through life."

He smiled. "I know. I have three sisters. They each put my mother through hell at one time or another. So now that there's a real possibility she may find her mother, you're thinking, who am I? Am I about to lose her?"

Mel nodded. "So much of how I define myself, so many of the choices I've made in my life, are tied to my being Tien's mother. I am in a totally different place than I imagined for myself thirty years ago. When I was working in Saigon I thought I wanted nothing else than to be a war correspondent, someone who could translate the reality, the horror, the underbelly of war."

"Any regrets that that's not who you are now?"

"None. I didn't understand then how deeply satisfying this life would be. So, no regrets. But costs – there have been costs."

"Like not being a war correspondent."

She nodded.

"Any others?"

She looked him in the eye, then reached into a deep part of herself.

"I didn't marry."

"Because of Tien?"

"I wanted a father for her as well as a husband for me. The man had to be both, and I didn't find him. What about you? What have the costs been for you?"

She waited, hoping that his willingness to listen to her and his perceptiveness about how vulnerable she felt would translate into a willingness to let down the mask.

"After I arrived in Cambodia I lost touch with everything and everyone who had meant something in my life. Including you."

"Why?" With this revelation of his she was no longer the objective reporter.

"I was captured and imprisoned. By the time I was released four years later, I'd lost faith in humanity, and in the God whose will I thought I was following. I descended into a dark and hopeless time in my life. I disappeared more thoroughly from those who loved me than when I had been in prison."

One of the aides from the clinic stood at the bottom of the veranda stairs.

"Doc, the men are starting to arrive for the clinic hours. Will you be down soon?"

He seemed relieved to stop the revelations. It occurred to Mel that he had buried this part of his life and never spoken about it to anyone else.

"Look, it's getting late to start down the mountain. Why don't you spend the night here at the compound? We have plenty of room. We can have dinner when the clinic hours are over and continue over conversation. In fact, do you want to shadow me at the clinic?"

Mel smiled, accepted the invitation, and followed him across the courtyard and up into the clinic.

The next two hours reminded her of the scenes she'd seen so many times at the orphanage. Phil bantered in Lahu as the men brought him their aches and pains, their faces lighting up as Phil bent to listen to their hearts or deftly probed a tender muscle. At times he turned to Mel to translate or explain – one man expressing worry about his son, who wanted to leave the village; another joking with Phil about his singing. Patients presented him with barter as payment – a scrawny white chicken, a net bag filled with cabbages, an embroidered cap, which Phil put on immediately.

What Mel witnessed was affection on both sides.

Dinner was communal, the entire staff at a long table in a large room in their quarters. Like Phil's house, it was on stilts with an open porch overlooking the mountain. Mel enjoyed the give-and-take of conversation and was surprised by Phil's rapport with them all. She had only known him as a loner, forgetting that he had once been a Marine. She had assumed he preferred to work on his own, not willing to engage in the compromise and balancing of everyone's needs that being part of a team required. But he seemed quite at home with the five people around the table.

After dinner people dispersed to their own pursuits and Phil invited her back to the veranda for a continuation of their conversation. He didn't seem ready to pick up where they had left off, so she asked a more comfortable question.

"What will you do with the MacArthur money?"

A wide grin stretched across his face, and she saw flickers of the energy and drive she remembered in the young Phil Coughlin.

"Oh, my God! Let me tell you what I'm going to do – operating rooms, more mobile clinics; fellowships to bring specialists here for short-term assignments."

He grabbed a sheet of paper and sketched out the new building he had planned. His excitement was undisguised. The grant had unleashed the restraint he had practiced for years trying to make do with the most limited resources. He could accomplish so much that he had only dreamed of doing in the past.

As the evening deepened so did their conversation, meandering from one topic to another and eventually returning to how he had pulled himself out of the darkness. He talked about how he had stumbled upon the need among the hill tribes and why he ultimately decided to stay; the evolution of what he was trying to accomplish; his realization that he was on a mission to which he was passionately committed.

In all of what he described to Mel there was one thing glaringly missing. Like her, he had never married.

"My mother, the devoutly Catholic Margaret Mary Daly Coughlin held out hope for awhile that I might enter the priesthood. In retrospect, what I've chosen to do with my life has been a kind of priesthood. I don't think one can do this without the kind of single-minded devotion you find in those who take vows."

"That single-mindedness is a two-edged sword," Mel interjected. "It's a strength, keeping us focused on the goal, but in the extreme, it also keeps us from letting anything or any*one* else share our attention."

They continued to talk. Late in the night, the sky overhead brilliant with stars, they reached the moment Mel referred to as the "crossing-over" point. The moment of true intimacy when the layers of disguise have been peeled away and one reveals one's deepest self. It was exhilarating and excruciating at the same time. For just as they bared their souls to one another and acknowledged what had occurred, they also realized that it was coming to an end. Morning was nearly upon them. Tien was waiting in Ho Chi Minh City; Sam was waiting for her article; the first of the patients were making their way up the mountain to the compound.

Phil wrapped her in an embrace as the first birds began their song in the trees below the veranda. They were emotionally spent; they had no more words. But they were friends.

Mel left the compound before the rest of the staff had awakened, her notebook full and her heart both joyful and bereft.

When she landed at Tan Son Nhat, Tien was waiting in the arrivals lounge with a driver and the address she'd been given by the Ministry. Mel understood the urgency, and despite her fatigue, didn't object when Tien told her she wanted to go immediately to Anh.

The car headed to the northern outskirts of the city to a district that had been open land when Mel had last been in Saigon. It came to a stop at a tall gate, beyond which Mel and Tien could see what looked like parkland. They were confused and thought the driver had the wrong address, but he pointed out the road sign and the number on the gate.

Mel and Tien climbed out of the car and approached the gate. It was Mel who realized first where they were. She reached out for Tien's hand as a soft moan escaped from her lips. Then, stepping ahead, they passed through the gate and into the cemetery. They followed a path of crushed white rock to the numbered row on the slip of paper that Tien had thought identified an apartment. When they reached the spot they found a polished stone set level with the earth.

Inscribed upon it was Anh's name, the years of her birth and death, and the inscription "Mother of Beloved Daughter Tien."

Tien knelt and touched the stone, tracing her own and her mother's names. Mel knelt beside her and enfolded her daughter close to her heart as Tien's tears began to fall, a curtain of water as steady as the monsoon.

When they returned to the hotel, Tien told Mel she wanted to go away for a few days. She had learned of a Buddhist monastery that offered retreats in Da Nang. Before they returned to the States she thought she needed time for solitude and meditation.

"I can leave this afternoon on a bus, if you don't mind."

"I'm fine. I have to write this profile for Sam and then I'm going to sleep for as long as I can. I think it's just what you need."

After she had seen Tien off on the bus, Mel holed up in her hotel room with her notebook, her laptop, and a carafe of tea. She typed nonstop for two hours composing a piece she called *Reckoning for a Lifetime: The Costs That Will Not Be Recompensed*.

The article began with a list, entitled "Expenditures for a Lifetime."

    1. 7 roundtrip tickets between Boston and Bangkok

    2. 25 Smith-Corona typewriter ribbons

    3. 272 cartons of Lucky Strike cigarettes

    4. 9 pairs of khaki shirts and shorts

    5. 17 pairs of Birkenstock sandals

    6. A lung

    7. A pediatric practice in Brookline, Massachusetts

    8. Anne Marie Reilly, who wrote to him through medical school and residency and the Marines and waited another two years for him to "get Southeast Asia out of his system," but who would not join him when he decided he could not leave

and so told Jimmy Lane that she would marry him.

9. 4 pairs of black plastic-framed eyeglasses

10. 7 cases of Glenlivet

11. 12 reams of 24-pound white Strathmore typing paper

12. A fully equipped field operating room

13. An army surplus Jeep

14. A rosary blessed by Father Joe Fallon, S. J., his high school buddy

15. Not being at his mother's bedside when she died of pancreatic cancer

16. 700 doses of penicillin

17. An M-16 rifle and 50 rounds of ammunition

18. A Zippo lighter

19. Galvanized tin to roof the clinic

20. One navy blue suit to wear when he spoke at fundraising dinners

21. Grey's Anatomy, the PDR and a surgery textbook

22. A Douay-Reims Bible

23. Children of his own

24. Lumber to build his mountain clinic

25. The ashes when rebels burned it to the ground

When she finished, she opened the French doors and sat on the balcony. It was dusk, and in contrast to the silence and beauty of the night before, the cacophony of Ho Chi Minh City greeted her just over the hotel's courtyard wall. She contemplated what she had just written and understood that to submit it for publication in the *Post* would be a betrayal of the trust Phil had placed in her.

She went back to the laptop, opened up her Gmail account and attached the article to an email addressed not to Sam but to Phil.

"This is yours," she wrote. "It belongs to no one else."

She'd write another profile for the *Post* in the morning. But first, she desperately needed sleep.

Despite the sounds and lights of the city, she fell into a deep sleep immediately, brought on not only by her physical exhaustion but also by the lightening of a burden. She'd given something back to Phil in return for what he'd given her the night before on his veranda.

In the middle of the night she was awakened by an insistent and disorienting sound. It took her a moment to recognize the ring of her cell phone. It was Phil.

"Where are you?"

She gave him the name of the hotel.

"Stay there."

She mumbled an agreement and then drifted back to sleep. Several hours later, still in bed, she heard the phone again and then a knock on the door.

"I'm here," he said.

She opened the door, the phone still at her ear.

"I've lost enough in my life. Now that I have found you again, letting you go is not a cost I'm willing to bear."

He reached out for her.

All the revelations from the night before flooded back and the emotional connection that had been forged between them suddenly was transformed into a physical one. Her body in its thin cotton nightgown molded itself to the solidity of his. He took her face in his hands and kissed her, his lips hungry and searching. He slid his arms down and slipped them under her, lifting her and carrying her back to the bed.

He saw that the other bed hadn't been slept in.

"Your daughter?"

"Away at a monastery," she murmured.

He sat by her side and she looked up at him.

"No one has ever understood me in the way you do. That article shook me to my core. How did you do that? How did you get me to reveal so much of myself?"

"I took a leap of faith."

"How so?"

"I thought if I offered to peel back a layer of my own, you might reciprocate."

"You were taking a risk."

"I know. But I wanted to know who you were. Not for the article, but for myself. I'd always found you so compelling and that frightened me. I wanted to overcome my fear by understanding who you were."

"And now you know."

"I know *part* of you. There is still more to explore and discover." She smiled as she began to unbutton his shirt.

He stretched out alongside her and kissed her again. Slowly, with great tenderness, they made love. For both of them it had been a long time since they had been with anyone. They savored every stage, holding back while they explored one another, delighting in the contours and hollows of each other's body, reveling in the tactile explosion of skin to skin. When they finally came it, was with a deep and vibrant satisfaction. Once again Mel slept, this time wrapped in Phil's arms, his lanky body spooned around her.

Later that day, after Mel had told him about finding Anh's grave, he asked what she and Tien would do next.

"After Tien returns from her retreat, I expect that we'll return to the states."

"How long will she be gone?"

"A few days, perhaps a week."

"So there's nothing to keep you here in Ho Chi Minh City until she returns."

"Only you."

"I can't stay. Even with the staff holding things together, I should return to the mountain. It's where I need to be."

Mel felt her heart constrict. She should have realized how ephemeral and impermanent these last few hours with Phil were. She'd conveniently ignored the reality of their divergent paths in life in the passion and wonder of rediscovering one another. She held back her disappointment that he would leave so soon. No regrets, she told herself. Even knowing that it was only this one night, she'd embrace it once again.

"I have a request," Phil said, stroking the side of her face.

"Come back with me while Tien is in Da Nang. You said yourself that I'm the only thing that keeps you here. You can write as easily on my veranda as you can in this room."

Her rational side cautioned her that it would be all the more painful to leave him if she went with him now, only postponing the inevitable. But she had forsaken caution when she opened up her life to him that first night on the mountain.

"I'll come." She took another leap of faith, trusting that whatever happened in the next few days could only enrich their lives, no matter in what direction each turned.

She sent word to the monastery, packed up and left Vietnam this time with Phil at her side.

The days she spent with him on the mountain deepened the emotional connection between them. In the evenings, she and Phil continued their conversations, delving into what had shaped and challenged them in the thirty years that had separated them. When she remarked that he no longer drank, he offered her the harrowing story of his descent into alcoholism and his subsequent climb to sobriety. In their bed at night their lovemaking captured what they had learned about one another, weaving their stories together in a way that bound them closer.

During the day when Phil was treating patients in the clinic Mel reached out to the Lahu women. Despite the language barrier, she was accepted into their circle, working beside them in the garden and learning to cook a vegetable curry spiced with galangal and chilies. Over the course of her stay she finished the new profile for the *Post*, a piece that she knew captured the complexity of the man and his work.

She wasn't sure if it was the altitude or the clarity of the air or the simplicity of village life, but she felt invigorated, healthier than she had in years. She also felt a satisfaction that she hadn't thought possible.

The end of the week loomed, and with it the pull of all the other threads in her life—her daughter, her work, her close-knit network of friends in Washington. Once again the rational voice intruded and she slipped into a contemplative, distant mood.

That night in bed, as Phil held her, he spoke aloud what neither of them wanted to face.

"When I came to you that night in Ho Chi Minh City, I told you I didn't want to lose you again. This week with you has only reaffirmed for me what you mean to me. I know I am asking something extraordinary of you—to give up the life you've built for yourself.   But I cannot bear to let you go this time. Be my wife."

All of the limitations and expectations that had defined her life up until that moment crowded into the darkened room, grasping for her. But she turned inward and listened to the voice that had barely been a whisper in Saigon thirty years before but now was strong and confident.

"Yes," she answered.

They made love, this time with an intensity and passion and understanding strengthened by the choice each had made to be with one another, a choice worth the cost.

The next morning Tien called to let Mel know she was ready to leave Da Nang.

"Fly to Chiang Mai," Mel told her. "I'll meet you there."

She picked Tien up at the airport and as they drove up the mountain listened to her daughter's experience at the retreat. She wasn't ready to share with Tien what had happened until she'd had the opportunity to introduce her to Phil in the village. But she was convinced that once Tien knew him, she would understand Mel's decision.

They arrived just before lunch, greeted by the soccer boys who escorted them to the dining room. After introductions, Tien got swept up into the lively conversation around the table and seemed at ease and at peace with herself.

When the meal was over, Phil walked Mel and Tien back to his verandah.

"I have something I want to show you, Tien," he said as he reached for a thick photo album on the table, its cheap plastic cover dry and cracked.

"It's a record of the final days of the orphanage."

"How did you manage to save the photos?" Mel asked, remembering Phil's capture and imprisonment in Cambodia after he left Saigon.

"I'd sent my mother the undeveloped rolls of film before I left Vietnam—a peace offering or a smoke screen, depending on how you look at it. I thought it would comfort her to see the children, knowing she was so worried about my decision to leave Boston. When I was imprisoned, the photos—and your *Newsweek* article—were all she had, so she put together the album. She saved it, and when she passed away my sisters found it and sent it to me."

Tien's eyes grew wide as she moved closer to Phil to view the album. There were photos of the villa and group shots of the different age groups of the children, all of which Tien studied carefully. Then Phil turned the yellowed page and showed her two photos, side-by-side. In the first, a baby in the arms of a young Vietnamese woman in a pale yellow ao dai.

"That is you with your mother Anh."

Tien bent over the page, gasping.

"She looks like me!"

"This is another photo of you with Anh and Melanie. I took it the day before the evacuation."

"This last item is the *Newsweek* article that sparked the Babylift.

"Your mothers saved your life, Tien. Both of them."

Tien looked across the table at Mel.

"I know that now," she said. She reached out to Mel and Mel embraced her daughter. At that moment Mel felt the same force that had flowed from Anh so many years before when she had entrusted Mel with her daughter's future, her daughter's life. That force was coming now from Tien, stronger as a result of her journey into the past and her acceptance of who both her mothers were and what they had done for her. Mel knew Tien would flourish; and she could tell from the perceptive, accepting expression in Tien's eyes as she looked at Mel and Phil that Tien would understand Mel's decision to marry Phil and join him in the mountains.

She wiped the tears from her eyes—tears of joy at all that she had regained on this journey—her daughter's understanding and Phil's love.

A Message from Linda Cardillo

Thank you for reading *Two Mothers*. I hope you enjoyed it! As an author, I am always gratified to hear from readers and deeply appreciate when you share your experience of the book—through a review on Amazon or Goodreads or simply spreading the word to your friends.

If you'd like to learn more about my books, read excerpts from new work and wander through my musings on the writing life, please visit my website and sign up for my newsletter at www.lindacardillo.com

I invite you to explore my other books.

About the Author

LINDA CARDILLO is an award-winning author of historical fiction and historical romance. She writes about the old country and the new, the tangle and embrace of family, and finding courage in the midst of loss.

She is also co-founder of Bellastoria Press, an independent publisher of compelling and beautiful stories.

In an earlier life Linda worked as an editor of college textbooks before earning an MBA at Harvard Business School at a time when women represented only 15% of the class. Armed with her Harvard degree, she managed the circulation of *Inc.* magazine during its successful start- up, founded a catering business and then built a career as the author of several works of nonfiction, from articles in *The New York Times* to books on marketing and corporate policy. Throughout her professional life and while raising her family, she nurtured her intention to write fiction. Her debut novel, *Dancing on Sunday Afternoons,* which launched Harlequin's Everlasting Love series, was published in 2007.

When she isn't writing, Linda loves to cook and is happiest when the twelve chairs around her dining room table are filled with people enjoying her food. She speaks four languages, some better than others. She plays the piano every night—sometimes by herself and sometimes in an improvisational duet with her younger son. She does *The New York Times* Sunday crossword puzzle in ink, a practice she learned from her mother. From her mother she also absorbed a love of opera, especially those of Puccini and Verdi, whose music filled her home when she was a child. She once climbed Mt. Kenya and has very curly hair.

For news and upcoming events, previews of new work, and musings on the writing life, sign up for Linda's newsletter at lindacardillo.com.